To: Bettye,
God bless you in
every way and always,
JOAN BAKER
2007

Ride the Dappled Mare

A Civil War Romantic Novel

Joan Elizabeth Moody Baker

DORRANCE PUBLISHING CO., INC.
PITTSBURGH, PENNSYLVANIA 15222

The contents of this work including, but not limited to, the accuracy of events, people, and places depicted; opinions expressed; permission to use previously published materials included; and any advice given or actions advocated are solely the responsibility of the author, who assumes all liability for said work and indemnifies the publisher against any claims stemming from publication of the work.

ISBN-10: 0-8059-7098-3
ISBN-13: 978-0-8059-7098-2
Library of Congress Control Number: 2005933631

Printed in the United States of America

First Printing

For information or to order additional books, please write:
Dorrance Publishing Co., Inc.
701 Smithfield Street
Third Floor
Pittsburgh, Pennsylvania 15222
U.S.A.
1-800-834-1803

Or visit our website and online catalogue at www.dorrancebookstore.com

Dedication

This book is dedicated to my granddaughter, Stephanie Brooke Baker, who has a vivid imagination and a talent for writing; and to my husband, Charles, the love of my life.

Foreword

"Lest we forget" are not idle words. They bespeak of past actions and experiences which are worthy of recall; actions which have affected individual lives and, in some instances, the involvement of nations. Such is the story told by the author in *Ride the Dappled Mare.*

The characters, placed in the Charleston, South Carolina area during the 1860's, find themselves totally immersed in the trials and tribulations of a conflict, which divided a young nation less than a century old. This is the story of a local judge, a pillar of the community, and his family with particular attention to his two charming daughters.

The reader will not find an archetypical Southern judge, as his viewpoint has a broader scope, which lends itself to principles beyond local politics. As a dedicated humanitarian, he is not passive. He has a devotion to duty and to seeing that justice is done for one and all. His loyalty is to family, friends, and nation. One becomes absorbed in the unfolding events on the plantation, the city, the river, and the battlefields. A very realistic picture is painted of compassion for everyone, not only the privileged.

One of the pleasures in reading this book is the artistic skill of the author as employed in Victorian descriptive presentations of both personalities and scenes. We meet well-developed characters with exposed traits — good and bad. A sympathetic view is easily acquired when influenced by vividly portrayed events, whether of thwarted love or effects of battle.

While excellently researched military facts are incorporated, the consequences of war are so intertwined into the story that they are not overwhelming. Both rich and poor, black and white, North and South, have times of problems and times of happiness.

As life continues during good and bad times, so does love; hence, the beautiful love story, which dances across these turbulent years of a young British gentleman and the Southern belle. Magnolias still bloom and honeysuckle still perfumes the air. Beauty, drama, tragedy; all human emotions find a home here.

— Josephine Miller

Acknowledgements

Sincere appreciation is expressed to Josephine Miller,
my mentor and encourager;
and also my love and gratitude to my husband, Charles,
for his patience in proofreading and editing the manuscript.

Chapter 1

The cannons in Charleston Bay spit out fusillades of hail throughout the night. Further inland, the church bells rang, arousing the sleepy countryside.

York Selassie awoke and stretched her taut muscles lazily. The sunlight, streaming through the Venetian lace curtains, papered the walls with incandescent light and pattern. The portrait of a beribboned child, sporting chestnut hair and dimpled cheeks, smiled back at her. York studied her older reflection in the mirror of the ornate wardrobe. Her hair fell loosely down her shoulders like a shimmering waterfall. She was gaining weight in all the right places. Today she was seventeen. She smiled. Her dimples deepened, then disappeared into a pall of sadness. An ebullition of emotion enveloped her.

These were not normal times — the North and South were on the verge of a civil war. The *Charleston Mercury* reported that an arms buildup by Union forces at Fort Sumter was imminent. York hoped this was only a rumor. She and her sister, Victoria, had spent many pleasant afternoons boating to Fort Johnson and Fort Sumter in the company of their father and Major Anderson. Was President Lincoln's real objective to preserve the Union, free the slaves, or despoil the South? All this and more, she could not answer.

York did not linger over her toilette, nor did she need to. Did she know that hers was a fresh, natural beauty that needed little embellishment? Swaddling herself in layers of petticoats and donning a white pelisse day dress, she retrieved her slippers and strolled out on the balcony of the stately Manor House.

From her "crow's nest" perch in the low country, she could see the Ashley River penciled across the greening landscape. Fields of rice and cotton, the latter known as "white southern gold," now lay fallow. How quickly nature, out of necessity, bursts forth and erases the past, she pondered. She watched a robin make a sneak attack upon an unsuspecting earthworm. A "tug of war" ensued. Was this what the skirmishes between the North and South were all about — a "tug of war," with the victor taking the spoils?...King Cotton, high and lifted up, enthroned upon the shoulders of slave labor; was it worth it all?

Her father and namesake, Judge Walter York Selassie, didn't think so. He had never owned a slave, but a number of slave families had sought refuge on the Selassie Plantation. He was reputed to be a dispassionate Judge and had helped many slaves to become freedmen. He believed in education for all (to the chagrin of the populace) and taught his well-paid sharecroppers how to read and write in their spare time. Most of his field hands were seasonal and had gone their separate ways except for the Lewis family: Mandy, Paddy, and their son, Aaron. They were not inclined to leave; therefore, the Judge retained them as domestic help. Now that his work load was more taxing and taking him farther and farther away from home, he spent less time on the plantation and more time pursuing his profession. Traveling cross-country and trying court cases left him little time for farming.

York didn't know what she and Victoria would have done without the Lewis family after their mother's death. She sighed. Pneumonia was no respecter of persons...time had dimmed, but not diminished, the memory of her beloved mother, Abigail Selassie.

Footsteps were heard on the landing. York could tell by the gait that it was the buxom Mandy.

"So, der you is, Missy York! You be up mighty early 'dis morning."

"Good morning, Mandy."

"Mornin', chile."

"My, my, you sho' do look purty. Yes ma'am, jus' a-standin' der in de' breeze, jus' like yo' mammy use' to."

"Really, Mandy, just like mama?"

"Dat's de truth, Missy, jus' like yo' mammy."

"Tell me about mama, Mandy."

"What you 'wanna' know, chile?"

"Everything, Mandy — everything!"

"Why jus' you look in de mirror, missy, dats' what yo' mammy was like. You be de spittin' image o' her. She was a looker, yo' maw...a mite too proud, but she had a good heart. She nursed my boy, Aaron, through dat' ole' devil, yellow fever. He be's pert' nere' gone when she come by de house, an' he be's a strappin' boy of eighteen now as I recollect."

"Oh, do go on, Mandy, tell me more."

"Well...Miss Abigail, she sho' luved' yo' pappy. See dat' road a-windin' down by de river?" Mandy paused to take in York's expression.

"Yo' maw' would see Mistah Walt a-comin', an' she knowed it was him by de way he be stirrin' up de dust to git to her."

York brightened; Mandy continued.

"It was like dis', you see," Mandy said in mimicry, "Miss Abigail would pat her hair, and slide her hands down de back side o' her dress dis' way, like as how she was a-smoothin' out de wrinkles an' all, an' when Mistah Walt git close, she would pinch her cheeks so's they be's pink an' all when de master come ridin' up. Many a-time I seen her a-standin' dere in de breeze, sho' nuff, Missy, early in de mornin' and late in de evenin', jus' like a shadow on de moon."

"Oh Mandy, that's so romantic...just like a shadow on the moon."

"Lawsy, Missy, you done gone an' made me forgit' what I done come up heah' for. Dat' sister of yo's, Miss Vicki, she all in a flutter dis' mornin'. Yo' pappy done come home 'fore de rooster crowed, an' brung' a han'some young gentl'man with him."

"A handsome young gentleman? Who is he, Mandy?"

"Best I recollect, he be's a Mistah Tray Hampton, de nephew of yo' pappy's friend, dat' other Mr. Hampton who be's from up Boston way. My man, Paddy, he say dis' youn'in be one of dem' high muckety-mucks, who done come down from de way of de mother country. He sho' do talk funny. Be dat' as it may, Miss Vicki, she all dressed in her best frock an' dat' new whalebone hoop skirt. She says you is to do de same."

"I do declare, Mandy, I should warn the gentleman. Victoria consistently bemoans the fact that she is nineteen and destined to remain an old maid." York only scoffed at her sister's dramatic theatrics. It was common knowledge that Victoria was the belle of Charleston society.

"Maybe she have cause now, Missy. Mos' gentl'men done left de country to jine' up wid' de Con-found-eracy."

York stifled a laugh. "That's Confederacy, Mandy, Confederacy."

"Yess'um, Con-found-eracy. Now jus' yo' git goin', chile', an' do what Miss Vicki says. She be's de eldest, an she rules de roost."

"I shall wear my prettiest frock, but I shan't wear that old hoop skirt that spins and twirls like a top every time I turn around and sit down. My petticoats will do just fine."

"Now, now, Missy, why you want to go an' ruffle Miss Vicki's feathers, seein' as how she be so happy dis' mornin'. Yo' mammy would'a worn her finest when folks come to call. Sides, Miss Vicki, she say dem' seven petticoats be's too hard to iron when de weather be's hot and muggy."

York realized the latter comment was more for Mandy's benefit than Victoria's, so she acquiesced.

"All right, I'll do as you say, but only until the big 'muckety-muck', as you call him, takes his leave."

"I don't figger' de gentl'man be leaving soon. He done gone an' got hiss self all beat up."

"Why, whatever do you mean, Mandy?"

"My man, Paddy, tole' me the gentl'man look a mess when he come in wid' yo' pappy 'for daylight dis' morning'. Some kinda trouble over at de boat landing."

"Well, I've never heard such happenings in the town of Charleston before."

"I reckon all dis' talk about war done got us all messed up, Missy. Can't tell no more who be's de friends and who be's de enemy. I best be gittin' back to de kitchen. Miss Vicki says we is

4

goin' to have a late breakfast for de men folks. I spect' de preacher be comin' long, too, soon's he smells de fat in de fryin' pan.
Lawsy me, I's don't know who I's feeling sorrier fur', de fat
preacher, or de horse dat' totes him."

"Sush, Mandy! You must not talk that way about the Rector.
Speaking of horses, I wanted to put the dappled mare through her
paces here in the cool of the day. Do you think you and Victoria
could manage without me this morning? It would only be for a
short while, and it *is* my birthday."

"Sho 'nuff?" Mandy stopped in her tracks and scratched her
pearly gray hair. "Why it sho' is, Missy, it sho' is. I be's forgittin'
you is a grown-up lady now. You ain't a'mindin' to see that
Johnny-Reb, Andrew Foy, over at de next plantation, is you?"

"Of course not! It wouldn't be prudent for a lady to call on a
gentleman unannounced, even if she wanted to."

"Well...suppose I tell my boy, Aaron, to saddle up yo' dappled
mare, an' den' tell Mis' Vicki you was outta yo' room."

"Oh, would you, Mandy? It would only be slightly deceitful,
for I am out of my room, am I not?"

"Sho' nuff, Missy, sho' nuff. But jus' you be back soon, an'
don't come a-walkin' in de big house a-smellin' like a piece-o'
horse flesh."

"Dear Mandy, whatever would I do without you?"

Mandy grunted in reply, and fanned her apron at York. "Now
git', chile', fore we-uns' both ends up in a heap o' trouble."

Chapter 2

Tray Hampton was restless. Sleep had left him, but he found himself drowning in a slough of despondency. The moral degradation he felt over the Confederate capture of his Uncle Hugh Hampton's merchant vessel, the *Parvenu*, and the attack upon his person by three burly hooligans in Charleston's harbor had left its mark. The cut over his right eye had ceased its throbbing, but the tell-tale signs of a bruise had manifested itself. Even though tensions were running high between the North and South, Tray had never experienced such disrespect and hatred. How could he have known that less than twenty-four hours before he crossed the bar into Charleston Bay, Confederate forces had attacked Fort Sumter. His quarters were searched, and he and the Shipmaster were not allowed to take anything ashore except a few personal items of clothing. It was futile to argue that no declaration of war had been announced by President Lincoln, for the rebels in South Carolina were bent on seizing all federal ships, forts, and arsenals within its borders. He could not defend his Uncle Hugh's trusts against such uneven odds. He shuddered.

He didn't know what might have happened if Judge Selassie had not intervened in his behalf. He mused at the Judge jumping right into the middle of the fight, wearing his austere, statesman-like black coat, and top hat. Someone recognized him and cried, "It's Judge Selassie, boys, let's get out of here!" He guessed he and the Judge got in a few good licks before the fight ended. It was

7

admirable of the Judge to go the second mile and offer him hospitality, as well as protection under the law.

Tray's eyes trailed around the dimly lit room of the Manor House. It was typical of the cavernous splendor of southern mansions. The decor was tastefully done, but decidedly feminine. He noted several artifacts around the room: a gold leafed vanity tray, costly perfume bottles, a bejeweled comb and brush set, and a lacquered music box. Discolored parchment bearing the initials "A. S." was lying loosely on a small curved desk. Tray realized he had been quartered in the bedroom of the beloved deceased, Abigail Selassie. He guessed the Judge's bedroom was next to this one, for there were double doors leading into the common water closet. A lace gown was peeking at him through a crack in the ornately carved wardrobe. He dared not open it for fear of stirring the ashes of memories that obviously and painfully had settled over the Selassie household.

Tugging at his bootstraps, he opted for an early morning walk to clear his head. He didn't know when the rebel's "seek and search" party would be over and he could board the *Parvenu* again. But at any rate, he would not allow himself to prevail upon the Judge's generosity any longer than necessary.

He didn't hear anyone stirring as he quietly slipped down the large curved staircase and out the wide French doors that opened to the lower verandah. Later in the day, he would try to send a post to Hampton Freight Lines in Boston, but news travels slowly in the South. He guessed he wasn't more than seven or eight miles out of Charleston, but he couldn't be certain. His Uncle Hugh was not going to take this delay lightly and there would be the "devil to pay" when word came to him that the whole crew had deserted the ship at the sound of á few rebel shots. Tray was satisfied that the captain and crew were all pretty well scattered and besotted with liquor by now. More than likely many of them were sleeping off their sins in the local brothels.

After walking some distance down the bridle path that meandered along the Ashley River, Tray shed his frock coat. He leaned back against a gnarled, old oak tree laden with moss. Mentally, he labeled it the "old man with the beard." The clement weather, coupled with the cool breeze and lapping of waves, cast a hypnotic spell over his brooding spirit. His whole body slowly began to relax, melding with the sights and sounds of nature at play. He felt as if he could stay there forever.

Looking back from whence he came, he observed the Negro man, whom Judge Selassie called Paddy, and his stalwart son, Aaron, milling about the carriage house and outbuildings. Presently, a stout Negro woman, emerged from the jaws of the big house, carrying a chamber pot in each hand. They all appeared to be moving in slow motion, but everything seemed to move in slow motion in the countryside of Charleston.

He didn't miss England as much as he thought he would, and he was not anxious to return to Boston, considering his latest decision to sever ties with Hampton Freight Lines. He knew his Uncle Hugh was grooming him for a prominent position in the mercantile business, as well as marriage to Dorthea Lyons of England. The Lyons were of noble descent, but the fair Dorthea was not exactly his "cup of tea." She was sickly and indulged. He could not allow the Lyons, or his uncle, to succor him into a loveless marriage, however advantageous it might prove to be. If and when he married, it would be to someone of his own choosing. He could never be happy fitting into Hugh Hampton's mold.

If the truth were known, all he ever wanted to do was study law. He remembered how his heart burned within him as he and Judge Selassie rode down the Ashley River Road and discussed all manner of legal science in the administration of justice.

Looking toward the East, he wondered what was happening in the Bay of Charleston. He didn't know what the future held for him, or the North and South, for that matter; he knew God held the future and — "May He help us all," he pontificated, "if Solomon's baby is cut in two!"

Tray thought he heard the drumming of a horse's hooves on the bridle path. He strained his ears to listen. The drumming slowed to a canter and he saw a sylphlike girl or young lady (it was hard to tell) riding a dappled mare. They picked up speed, left the bridle path, and gracefully jumped a low-lying fence. After circling the field several times, she reigned her horse in his direction. She was riding toward him at a healthy clip.

Had she seen him? He thought not. Realizing he had possibly invaded her privacy, he concealed himself behind the "old man with a beard." She was quite an accomplished rider. He gaped at her in admiration; she was innately beautiful, this "Daughter of the Limber-Lost" ...her hair and skirts flirting with the breeze.

As horse and rider drew near, the mare picked up Tray's scent, whinnied, bolted upright and deposited the girl on the ground. Tray paled. He was aghast! His presence had more than likely spooked her horse. He rushed to her side, apologizing profusely. "Oh do forgive me, my dear girl. I'm so sorry. I had no idea the calamity that was about to befall you. Are you all right?"

York was momentarily winded and could not speak. Satisfied that no bones were broken, Tray lifted her in his arms. She was light as a feather, and the close proximity of her body sent a wave of heat throughout his. How could skin so soft to the touch feel like a branding iron against his chest?

"I fear it is only my dignity that has been shattered," York replied, after recovering her speech. "Please put me down."

Tray was reluctant to do so.

"Please put me down," she said firmly.

He set her on her feet.

"Oh do forgive me, my lady. I must have taken leave of my senses," he stammered.

"I shall indeed forgive you, but I doubt if my horse, Duchess, ever will." The mare eyed Tray surreptitiously and pawed the ground.

"Then promise me you will allow me to redeem myself by calling on you at a more convenient time."

"I shall do nothing of the sort." York stiffened, then masked her smile. She noted the cut and bruise over his eye. So... this must be Mr. Tray Hampton, the high "muckety-muck," as Mandy called him. High muckety-muck, indeed...!

She decided to banter with him.

"Are you aware, Sir, that I am a daughter of the South, and that we are at enmity with the North?"

Tray decided to match her mood. He stepped back a few paces and bowed low.

"I was under the impression that President Lincoln had not declared war as yet, my lady."

"Even so, Sir, I hasten to inform you that you have crossed over into enemy territory, and this is private property."

"Yes, well...I do believe I must have strayed too far away from the Selassie Manor House. I shall vacate the premises immediately, if my lady wishes it."

"That is good, Sir. I shan't relish the idea of explaining to my Father that a 'Yankee' stranger has 'dared' to cross our borders."

"A Yankee tradesman by choice, an Englishman by birth, and a gentleman I might add." Tray decided to test her fortitude. "'Tis a pity your ladyship is too young to notice, and too old to act like a prig."

"You will forgive me Sir, if I withhold the olive branch, for that crude remark has just cost you the war!"

"So be it! But I warn you, lest you think me a 'popinjay,' I don't surrender easily, and I usually win."

"Oh really, now!"

"Yes. And perchance I should lose the battle, it will be a pleasant captivity, for never have I held a more beautiful Southern Belle in my arms."

"I do believe, Sir, that you seek to infiltrate our ranks through flattery."

"Oh no, my lady, I do not 'intend' anything of the sort. I am going to storm the Citadel," he teased.

"You will do so at great risk."

"I assure you, it will be well worth the risk."

"Very well, Sir, consider yourself forewarned." York turned her back on him and gracefully mounted the dappled mare.

Her "Sir's" sounded like "Suh's." Tray thought she was charming. He was loath to see her leave. "One moment, please."

York paused.

"There is one thing a soldier learns in battle, my lady, and that is never to turn one's back upon the enemy."

York turned around, cocked her head, and flashed him a winsome smile. "A gentleman wouldn't shoot a lady in the back, would he?"

Her smile was "dead-reckoning"...straight through the heart...a smile of victory. He was totally captivated with her.

"Let's hope our morning coffee has not grown as cold as our conversation," York cajoled. "I shall see you at half past nine. Welcome to the Selassie Plantation, Mr. Hampton!"

Tray reddened. York tossed her curls, clapped the reins, and disappeared around a bend in the river road. When she resurfaced, he saw her reining the mare in the direction of the carriage house.

So...she was one of the Judge's daughters...but which one? He had been duped and disarmed.

He chalked up one for the South!

Chapter 3

It was said of Judge Walter York Selassie, that no one ever left his table empty of mind or body, and today was no exception. Mandy had laid a commodious table. Breakfast consisted of a variety of sweet breads, cheese grits, eggs, thick slabs of bacon, and hot steamy biscuits. There were also flapjacks with butter, dark thick molasses, and fresh milk. The coffee was rich and aromatic, teasing the nostrils and warming the throat.

The Judge was of the opinion that if a man ate a hearty breakfast, the other meals didn't matter so much. After sailing from England for many days and eating ship biscuit (a fancy name for hardtack) Tray Hampton concurred. He thought he (along with the Apostle Paul) had been elevated somewhere between Eden and the Third Heaven. Such splendor! Such delicacies! And, all served on a bed of white linen, with crested china and silver utensils which caught the light.

There was quite an assemblage of guests around the table. Judge Selassie introduced his two daughters, Victoria and York, before properly introducing the others. Victoria Selassie was stunning in her own right, but it was York to whom Tray's eyes strayed. She gave no indication to her Father, or the others, that they had met earlier on the bridle path. He followed suit, and for that, he hoped she was grateful.

Among the guests were Reverend Jonas White, Rector of the Protestant Episcopal Church; Penelope and Clarissa Morgan of

New Orleans, the Judge's widowed sister and niece, respectively; Hattie Comstalk, the local school mistress; and Colonel Bates from the Federal Arsenal. Hattie Comstalk was a temporary boarder at the Manor House and Tray learned that Mr. Comstalk, while not in attendance, was employed by the Charleston and Savannah Railroad. During the course of the meal, Mrs. Comstalk confided to Tray that she and Mr. Comstalk were somewhat estranged. She boldly stated that there were some things a proper lady should not have to put up with, and Mr. Comstalk's drinking habit was one of them. Tray liked her, except for her prattling manner of speech.

Colonel Bates steeled his eyes on Mr. Hampton, sizing him up. Tray was no slouch...tall, aristocratic, impeccable in dress...but, he was too high-nosed to suit Bates. The Colonel didn't like the way Victoria was fawning over him.

It was rumored that Colonel Bates was in danger of losing his storekeeper's position at the Union arsenal because of his southern sympathies. The Colonel was courting Victoria, in hopes of extracting a pledge of marriage from her in the not-too-distant future. Judge Selassie had some reservations concerning the match; Colonel Bates had fought in the Mexican War when he was young, and there was quite a difference in his age and Victoria's.

The Judge thought his girls looked unusually bright and beautiful this morning. His niece, Clarissa, was no great beauty, but she had a sweet, amiable disposition that would carry her far. He called upon the Rector to offer a prayer of thanksgiving for the food. The Rector waxed eloquent on the trials and tribulations of the nation and invoked the almighty God's blessing and protection over the South, denigrating all Federal interference into the affairs of the Southern States by "blackguards," who had ascended straight from the pit of hell, etcetera, etcetera...

York wondered how the Rector could be so sure the Lord was on the side of the South. The food was getting cold, and she wished Reverend White would remember that he was not on trial before the Reviewing Board of the Protestant Episcopal Church. After the prayer, the men's conversation inevitably centered around the firing on Fort Sumter.

Penelope Morgan and Hattie Comstalk were discussing the pros and cons of the Abolitionists' movement. Penelope had the ability to listen to two conversations at once without slacking her speech.

"Fort Sumter?" She interposed to her brother, "Oh Walt, I do hope that nice Major Anderson and his men will be safe. Imagine being surrounded by rebels with no reinforcements in sight. I admire bravery on *both* sides, the North as well as the South, but it seems such a tragedy that the Union has seemingly abandoned these poor men to such an unfavorable destiny."

"It appears to be that way, Penelope, but let's hope that's not the case. If Union Major Anderson and General Beauregard can reach a compromise soon, no reinforcements from the Federal Government will be necessary."

"There won't be a compromise, Walter, if the Governor has anything to do with it," Colonel Bates replied. "Let's just hope he is not as mule-headed as some folks say he is."

"I spoke to the Governor about this matter, Colonel. I warned him that if he made a move toward Major Anderson at Fort Sumter, it would surely be viewed as an act of war by the Federal Government. I hardly see how the Union could turn the other cheek this time. The South would then stop at nothing to gain advantage over the Northern States. And may I be quick to point out that I am a southern gentleman who is not anxious for a wider war. I say, if we here in the South are bent on bloodshed, we should stop and count the cost before drawing our wagons in a circle."

"Well said, Walter, but whether you are ready for it or not, it's here," the Colonel responded. "It's time to realize that we all must choose between friend and friend. We can't straddle the fence much longer."

The Rector winced and shuffled in his chair. "Well...Colonel Bates," he drawled, "suppose reinforcements from the United States are forthcoming, who do you think stands the better chance of winning this war, the North or the South?"

"I can't say for sure, but the southern soldier is a better fighter. I learned this in the Mexican War; however, the North has greater resources than the South."

The Rector's big frame squirmed uneasily in his chair. "It seems to me the North is trusting more in might, than right."

15

"Could be, but some folks say England is on the side of the South. What do you say, Walter?"

"Let's address that question to Mr. Hampton. He just arrived from England; perhaps he has more of an insight into which way the political wind blows."

Tray looked up with a start. He was surprised and flattered that the Judge thought his opinion worth expressing, considering his youth and the gravity of the question.

"Sir," he answered carefully, "I...I am of the opinion, that if there is a wider war, England will remain neutral."

The Judge appeared to be pleased with Tray's evaluation.

"I disagree, Mr. Hampton." Colonel Bates felt as if he had already been upstaged socially by this young upstart, and he was not going to allow him to gain political prowess as well. "England desperately needs the South's cotton for their mills. Closed mills mean lost wages for mill owners. I don't think England would take too kindly to that. I'll wager they will fight for the South, and do it expediently!"

"But the people of Europe need northern wheat as well, Sir. I would venture to say that England is not ready to risk another war with the United States. With all due respect, Colonel Bates, and contrary to what some folks may believe, the European Nations have not yet recognized the Confederacy as an independent nation."

"They very well better recognize it as an independent nation, young man, for I tell you, the Confederacy is a force to be reckoned with!"

The Judge felt as if the conversation was heating up, so he changed the subject. "Gentlemen, gentlemen. All of this political debating is bound to unnerve our fair ladies here, so I would like to propose a toast to my lovely daughter, York, on her seventeenth birthday."

"Hear, hear! I'm all for that," Penelope Morgan chimed in. York blushed.

The celebration was upstaged by a loud, harsh knock on the parlor door. Glasses froze in mid-air. Tensions were high. Judge Selassie arose from the table; perhaps it was the latest news of the firing upon Fort Sumter.

It was.

With no relief in sight, and only a handful of wounded and hungry men, Major Anderson had surrendered to the Confederate forces at Fort Sumter! Would this be the catalyst that would start a civil war?

York did not fail to see the look on her Father's face.

For Walter York Selassie, it was a hollow victory.

Chapter 4

The next morning a storm was brewing. Paddy lit the outdoor gas lamps earlier than usual. "If de wind blows for three days, de rains am goin' to come," Paddy called out. York acknowledged him and strained against the wind to close the wide plantation shutters. He was right; the rains came.

Walter Selassie left home in order to carry provisions to his old friend, Major Anderson, and his starving soldiers in Fort Sumter. They had fought a good fight and he and many of the townspeople felt as if it was only fitting and right that they allow them to return to New York with dignity. Tray Hampton was advised not to accompany him considering the political arena in Charleston at this particular time. Tray spent most of his time in the Judge's library, leaving it only to appear at mealtime or to retire to his bedroom at night. Victoria was nonplussed. She couldn't understand how anyone could abide reading musty old law books all day; however, York was relieved. Her modesty told her it was better this way. Victoria intercepted her in the hallway and thrust a tray in her hands.

"York, would you take this tray up to Mrs. Comstalk? You know how she likes her afternoon tea in her room, and I can't find Mandy anywhere. I do declare, that woman can disappear at the most inopportune time. If you see her, tell her to fetch some clean linens for Mr. Hampton's room."

"That's Mother's room."

"Please, York, you're such a sour grape these days. You can't go on living in the past forever."

Victoria was right of course, but she found solace in fondling her Mother's things. Sometimes she imagined that her Mother was only away for a little while. The smell of her perfume seemed to linger in the room.

Victoria read York's thoughts. Occasionally, a tender moment was shared between them. "I know, Sis, I miss her, too," Victoria empathized. In an effort to cheer them both, she asked, "Why don't we accompany Aunt Penelope and Cousin Clarissa to the railway station tomorrow? We could go to market afterward."

"I would like that, Victoria."

"Perhaps Mr. Hampton would also like to ride into town with us — don't you think he is simply dashing, York?"

"Imposing, one must admit; but in my opinion, Mr. Hampton is pompous and assuming."

"You are being very unfair, York. Mr. Hampton is a paradigm of perfection. I simply adore his smile and eloquent mannerisms, and I do believe he is quite taken with my person."

"Proceed with caution, Victoria. Mr. Hampton has been at sea much too long without the company of a woman. Excuse me, I have work to do."

"I do declare. I will never understand that girl as long as I live," Victoria whispered beneath her breath.

York didn't know why she felt impelled to distance herself from Tray Hampton. Even so, that was no reason to be so curt with Victoria. Perhaps it was Mr. Hampton's blue-gray eyes that penetrated the veneer of her sensibilities...he affected her emotionally, and challenged her intellectually.

With Andrew Foy, it was different. Andrew was boyishly bashful and quiet — giving much, expecting little. He was a loyal friend. Why was he so quick to join up with the Confederacy...was it what he wanted, or was it merely peer pressure? She hated war — severing families, friends, and cutting a nation in two.

York carried Mrs. Comstalk her tea and looked in on her Aunt Penelope and Cousin Clarissa. She offered her assistance in helping them pack their trunks.

"Oh no, my darling," her Aunt Penelope protested. "We have almost finished packing, and Clarissa and I have everything we need. You and Victoria have been such dears. I'm afraid it may be some time before we will return, but you must come to New Orleans soon."

"Oh please do," Clarissa agreed. "There is so much to do there. We have parties and balls almost every night, and I'm sure I could find a proper suitor for you — someone like Mr. Hampton, perhaps. Isn't he just ravishing, York?"

"Now, now, Clarissa, you must not make bold your promises," her mother chided, "for I dare say, there is scarcely a young man in New Orleans who can hold a candle to Mr. Hampton in articulation and refinement. Of course, he could use a little fattening up, I suppose."

So...Cousin Clarissa, Aunt Penelope, and Victoria were all taken with Tray Hampton's person. Well, she was not going to feed his egotistical appetite...no, she was too sensible for that. Men like Mr. Hampton have a tendency to form a lofty opinion of themselves and rarely regard the feelings of the opposite sex, she concluded; but she managed to hold her tongue and did not express her feelings openly.

Chapter 5

"It's political chicanery! Political chicanery, that's what it is!" Judge Selassie had returned home.

As York passed by the library, she heard her Father's voice raised in anger. She could hear the nervous slapping of his crop against his thigh. He was a gentle man, and this outburst seemed so out of character for him. The door was slightly ajar, and she caught a glimpse of Tray Hampton with his back to the door. There was no mistaking his voice.

"Sir, as the Lord is my witness, and I can go no higher, to my knowledge Hampton Freight Lines has never dealt in contraband!"

Lest her father think she was eavesdropping, York hurried on down the hallway. They must have heard her footsteps, for there was a soft click on the library door. The words, "political chicanery" and "contraband," echoed in her ears. Was her father's anger aimed at Tray Hampton, or another? York could not temper her thoughts. Nothing made sense anymore, the war, Tray Hampton, or her father's increasing involvement in the war.

Later that evening when all the guests had retired, Judge Selassie summoned Victoria and York to the parlor. "Victoria...York, I had wanted to spare the two of you from any unpleasantness, but I feel as if the time has come for us to sit down together and discuss some vital issues that will affect all of us as a family."

The ominous tone of his voice was disconcerting.

"What's wrong, Father?"

"It's not a matter of wrong, Victoria, but a matter of right. Please listen carefully, both of you. Because of recent developments, I may very well deem it necessary to cease administering justice under the laws of the United States Government within the State of South Carolina."

"I don't understand, Father; what are you trying to tell us?" Victoria was puzzled. "He is saying," York explained, "that the time has come to choose between friend and friend. You heard it first from the lips of Colonel Bates."

"You are perceptive, York, but that is not all. Believe me, I have no choice in the matter. I must give an accounting to a much higher authority — the Almighty God! I took an oath before Him to uphold the laws of the United States Government; laws of which I cannot easily trample in the dust of a divided nation, under the guise of states' rights."

"But Father, what will you do?" Victoria asked. "How then shall we live?"

"We will manage, Daughter. I have not quite sorted it all out in my mind yet. I sought to prepare you both for change. Perchance, change is inevitable; it may possibly mean leaving our beloved State of South Carolina."

"Leave South Carolina? South Carolina — this house — our friends?"

"Would you mind so terribly, Victoria?"

"Oh yes, Father, yes! I will never leave South Carolina." Victoria ran upstairs to her room, closed the door and fell across her bed sobbing.

Walter Selassie wilted. Everything had not gone as he expected. York studied his face. She, too, wanted to give vent to her feelings, but the pained look in her Father's eyes restrained her. She had long suspected the struggle he was going through.

"Oh, Father," she exclaimed, jumping up and embracing him, "What does it matter where we live? We have each other don't we? That's all that counts, isn't it?"

"How like your Mother you are, my sweet York. If she were here now she would know what to do." He heaved a sigh. "Do see to your sister's comfort."

"Victoria will be all right, Father. She has been petulant ever since Mr. Hampton arrived."

"What has Mr. Hampton got to do with this?"

"Surely you must know she is totally enamored with him?"

"Victoria and Mr. Hampton?"

"Oh, *he* isn't aware of it, yet. In fact, he seems to be somewhat aloof and withdrawn of late."

"I'm not surprised. Mr. Hampton has his own brand of trouble right now."

"Trouble, Father?"

"It appears that he is innocently caught up in a political triangle between the North, the South, and England. All are laying claims to the cargo of Hampton Freight Lines. The Confederacy has labeled Hampton's goods contraband. It fully smacks of piracy if you ask me."

York's conscience was pricked. She had been less than cordial to Mr. Hampton. Could she have misjudged him?

"Is there anything you can do to help him, Father?"

"I don't know, York. We will have to be patient. You have heard it said that the wheels of justice grind slowly; nevertheless, they do grind. I have written the Secretary of the Navy about this matter. Meanwhile, Mr. Hampton will have to remain in my charge until we can traverse the proper channels. I hope his stay here won't be too much of an inconvenience for you and Victoria."

"Of course not, Father." Even as she said this, she knew in her heart that she had been inconvenienced quite enough simply by his manly presence. "We will have to make some adjustments, that's all."

"Yes, I've been thinking about that. I'm planning on quartering Mr. Hampton in the carriage house. I believe he would be more comfortable there than in Abigail's room, with all those feminine gewgaws hanging around. He tells me he is studying law and would welcome my tutelage. He's a fine young man. He will make a fine barrister some day."

Chapter 6

York had not been away from the plantation for some time and she was looking forward to escorting her Aunt Penelope and Cousin Clarissa to the train station, and shopping in Charleston. She regretted that they could not stay for the summer; she feared ennui would set in around the plantation after they were gone.

"Scuse' me, Missy York," Mandy interrupted, "but dat' Johnny-Reb, Andrew Foy, has come to call. He be's powerfully in a hurry to see you."

York knew Andrew had really come to say good-bye and to court her father's favor. His joining up with the Confederacy had been a bone of contention between them, but she must take it all in stride.

Andrew seemed older than his eighteen years in his gray cadet uniform with its turned down collar and brass buttons, glistening in the sunlight. His hair was shorn, and only a single red ringlet falling over his forehead was left to testify of his former crowning glory. York told him he looked nice in his uniform; yet, it made her sad.

"The war has spoiled it for all of us, hasn't it, York?"

"I must admit I was taken back by your actions, Andrew. Why did you enlist?"

"I didn't want to. It just happened, that's all."

"But you had a choice."

"Maybe I did, maybe I didn't. Father said that a man who is not willing to fight for his state is not worth his salt. I'm not a proud man, York. I have never been esteemed in my father's eyes. I thought this is what he wanted."

"What must your mother be feeling now? You are her only son."

"Mother said that if there is a wider war, I am not to come home unless we've won it."

"Andrew! I don't believe it."

"It's true. Mother is a staunch patriot of the South. She would enlist and bear arms herself, if that were possible."

"Oh, Andrew, I am so sorry."

"I have no right to ask you, York, but would you be my girl and write to me often?"

"Of course I'll write you, Andrew."

"I would be pleased if you would think kindly of me," he said shyly.

"I'm very fond of you, Andrew. We will be friends forever, I promise you."

Friends forever.... His countenance fell. He never was good with words.

Andrew wanted more; he wanted to love her and have her love him back. He wanted her for his bride. He wanted York! Must he settle for "friends forever?"

Chapter 7

Paddy and Aaron skillfully drew the horses and the carriage alongside the railroad platform. A small band of young men and boys sized up the drivers in their bright red waistcoats, black breeches, and top hats. Assuming that their black brothers had attached themselves to a white family of no small means, they pressed the doors of the carriage so tightly that it was impossible for Tray Hampton and the fashionable young ladies to exit.

"Well, I never!" Penelope Morgan exclaimed. "It's every bit as bad as the streets of New Orleans."

"Yes," Victoria replied. "Begging has become all too common here in Charleston. I suppose they are freedmen, unattached and hungry."

"Then we must pity them," York remarked. She would have emptied her purse then and there had not Aaron and Paddy taken charge. Paddy threatened to beat the hooligans within an inch of their lives if they did not back away to give the passengers room. He didn't have to warn them twice; they quickly dispersed.

"These not be yo' regular freedmen, Miss York. These be trouble-makers sho' nuff. I knows one of um.' I seen him hangin' round de boat docks a-beggin' for money and a-scarin' de' daylight outta' folks, what with dat' big frame o'his. He not scare me none. He be's lazy, dat' one. Now watch yo' step ladies, de' horses done got jittery."

Tray Hampton proffered his hand to the ladies. The baggage attendants hoisted the Morgans' trunks over the platform and Tray ushered the ladies up the steps to the train. The whistle blew and they boarded. There were tears, embraces, and white handkerchiefs flying among the spectators. The air was charged with excitement, and the noise and the hustle and bustle were unnerving.

Tray inquired of the latest war news from a gentleman standing nearby. He learned there had indeed been a buildup of arms and manpower in the New England States. This would surely mean a full-scale war between the North and South.

They all stood by and watched the "Puffy Dragon" until it was but a speck on the horizon. "Oh, do not let us stand here all day," Victoria remonstrated, "There is a lovely chocolatier a short distance from here that makes the most divine candy. Mr. Hampton, you must join York and me for refreshments before we do our marketing."

"But Victoria," York urged, "perhaps Mr. Hampton has business elsewhere. I'm satisfied he would rather follow more interesting pursuits in attendance with male company."

Tray did indeed have business elsewhere, but he had been advised by Judge Selassie to avoid any contact with his crew or the local authorities. "On the contrary, Miss Selassie. What better pursuit could I avail myself of than to escort two beautiful and charming young ladies around town. I'll wager I will be the envy of Charleston society."

"I do declare, Mr. Hampton, you do have a way with words," Victoria gushed.

York was not entirely satisfied with this arrangement, for it was ever so droll having a man looking over one's shoulder when viewing feminine frills, froufrou, and furbelows.

Nevertheless, it proved to be a profitable day. Before their shopping tour had ended, York had managed to purchase a book of verse for herself, cotton yardage for Mandy, tatting thread for Mrs. Comstalk, and a brass belt buckle for Aaron. She had bought nothing for her Father as yet, and only a small tin of licorice sticks for Paddy. Victoria had purchased chocolates, gloves, and a golden lavaliere to wear to the annual charity ball that was to be held at the Citadel a few weeks hence. York had not decided if she would be in attendance or not. It wouldn't be quite the same without Andrew as her escort.

Along the drive home, York drew out her book of verse and began to read. She was having a hard time interpreting *Shakespeare's Sonnets*, but the words printed on parchment, and beautifully illuminated, held a fascination for her, and she was determined to master its contents. It had not gone unnoticed that Victoria pressed Mr. Hampton's shoulder more than was necessary around the curves of the Ashley River Road. York thought her sister's behavior shameful; and she began to read in earnest. Occasionally, she would forget and look up, only to meet Mr. Hampton's stare. Needless to say, she was glad when the Manor House loomed into sight.

She would have so much to tell Andrew when she penned her first letter to him. She would not fail to mention the patriotic citizens of Charleston, the fireworks, and the crowded streets. She would tell him about all the bright young men in Confederate uniforms, and how they tipped their hats toward her Father's carriage as they rode by. Perhaps on a more mellow note, she would tell him how sweet the countryside smelled and how the birds were strangely silent in his absence...no, never would she be so bold as to voice the latter to Andrew. When she wrote to him, she would tender her speech in such a manner neither to encourage his fondness for her, nor jeopardize their friendship. Whatever she felt for Andrew, she knew it wasn't love.

The shadows grew long over the Ashley River Road and darkness veiled the sun. The cry of a whippoorwill pierced the night!

Chapter 8

*D*ear Miss York,

I have been informed by your benevolent sister,
Victoria, that you are reluctant to attend the charity
ball at the Citadel in Mr. Foy's absence.
I hither-to-fore am offering my services as your escort.
It would give me great pleasure to be in attendance
with you. Please consider this my proud and humble
service.

Sincerely,
Tray Hampton

Dear Mr. Hampton,
    Your proud and humble service,
    I do scorn,
    When upon another's wishes it is borne.

    Sincerely,
    York Selassie

York was certain Victoria would have been Mr. Hampton's first choice for an escort to the charity ball, had not Colonel Bates already engaged her. Victoria's motives were not entirely honorable, as York well knew. Colonel Bates was suave around the ladies, but he was not fond of dancing. Victoria had booked Mr. Hampton for every dance but two. This would surely fan the flames of Colonel Bates's jealousy. York did not want to be manipulated by her sister or Mr. Hampton.

"Father, you simply must talk to York."

"What seems to be the problem, Victoria?"

"She is as stubborn as a wild stallion. She refuses to go to the charity ball in Andrew's absence, and her behavior toward Mr. Hampton borders on insolence."

"Insolence?"

"Yes. She is rude and flippant with Mr. Hampton, and treats him with utter contempt at times. I fear she is lacking in social graces."

"I have not noticed York lacking in social graces."

"But Father, there's more — Mrs. Comstalk said York refuses to attend her elocution exercises. And just the other day, I saw her shed her petticoats, kick them behind our hedge row, and mount the dappled mare. I can't image what our guests would think if they saw York exposing her limbs and pantaloons in such an unladylike manner."

Walter Selassie smothered his laughter in deference to Victoria.

"Don't worry your pretty head, Victoria. York is like a young calf out of the stall. She will be muzzled soon enough."

"But, Father, she is no longer a child. How do you expect me to make a lady out of York if you don't discipline her?"

"I will talk to her, Victoria, I promise." Walter Selassie only winked at York's shortcomings. She was bright, viable, and vivacious — traits he highly admired in a woman.

He was tired. There were other weightier matters that needed his immediate attention. How was he going to tell his old friend, Hugh Hampton, that all hope of recovering the ship and cargo of Hampton Freight Lines was lost unless a letter from the Secretary of the Navy or Treasury was soon forthcoming?

President Lincoln had declared a blockade of all southern ports, and the war was escalating. With the attack on Fort Sumter, more states were prompted to join the Confederacy. A call had been sent out to southern plantation owners to offer up their slaves to help fortify the coastal and harbor defenses. Richmond had been named the capital of Virginia; the Confederate forces were on the offensive against the Army of the Potomac, and were confident that they would win.

Judging from the sheer manpower of the North, Walter Selassie feared the Confederates would eventually be turned back even if their initial attack was successful. His loyalty to the Confederacy was waning, and he was leaning toward the North. He knew this was driving a wedge between himself and his long time associates. He was fast losing popularity with the South. He had bucked the system by denouncing slavery, standing up for women's rights, and touting the preservation of the Union. Colonel Bates was right — he could no longer straddle the fence.

Judge Selassie did not sleep that night. His lamp burned until the first ray of light extinguished it. Finally, he drew a quill from his desk drawer and dipped it into the liquid darkness of the inkwell.

"Oh, Abigail," he whispered, "my Abigail... I've just stepped down from the bench. May God rest my case."

~ ~ ~ ~ ~

The following morning, the long awaited post from Hugh Hampton finally came. To say he was upset would be an understatement; he was livid... "Save the ship and cargo at all cost!"

Walter Selassie was grave. "Tray, my boy, I am doing all that is within my power to secure the release of your Uncle Hugh's merchant vessel."

"And I vouchsafe, Sir, this deed will not go unrewarded. We at Hampton Freight Lines will be eternally grateful for any assistance you might render us."

"I'm afraid it's not going to be that easy. I have not yet heard from the Secretary of the Navy or Treasury. Now as far as I can determine, the ship and cargo are still intact. I cannot vouch for

35

the crew. From what I have been apprised, there is some private profiteering going on. Letters of marque and reprisal have been issued by President Jefferson Davis allowing seizure of all northern ships at sea, and considering the ship *Parvenu* is held under lease to England, the Confederacy has put itself in quite a precarious position."

"I was under the impression that the Declaration of Paris signed by the European nations in 1856 protected us from private profiteering."

"You are partly right; however, the United States did not sign that declaration. It was most unfortunate that you arrived at Port Charleston on the heels of the firing upon Fort Sumter. All this political haranguing between England, and the North and South, has the whole judicial system tied up in knots. All are laying claim to the ship's cargo. It could take months, or years, before this matter is settled, and I predict the Lion of England will roar if the meat is snatched away from her cubs."

"What recourse do we have, Sir?"

"Very little, I'm afraid."

Tray's face fell. As Purser of the ship, he felt like a boy sent to do a man's job, and failing at every turn. A curse was on his lips, and it would have exploded, had he not checked his tongue. "I'll find a way out of this, Sir. I must!"

Walter Selassie's palms began to sweat. He had grown quite fond of Tray Hampton. There was another way, but he was hesitant to suggest it. "There is another recourse, my boy, but it's a dangerous one."

"Please tell me of it, Sir. Perhaps it is just youthful boasting, but I have faced danger before."

"You could run the blockade."

"Run the blockade?" Tray's heart quickened. He thought about it for a moment, and his spirits began to soar. "Of course...it had not crossed my mind to...yes...yes...I bloody well could, couldn't I?"

"It's a risky business, but the way I've got it figured, the longer you wait, the more Confederate pickets will be out there."

"What would be my chances of succeeding?"

"Well, the way I see it, this is mostly a paper blockade right now. On a dark, foggy night, and with a high tide at the bar, I would say your chances are good in getting out of the bay area. With the help of a few key people, and some of my friends in high places, I believe we could pull it off successfully. Captain Cromwell over at Fort Johnson has had experience in blockade running. I would like for you to meet him and discuss this matter further before you make your final decision. If you decide to run the blockade, I'm with you all the way, but of course, in open water you would be on your own. You realize we must keep this in the strictest of confidence."

"By all means, Sir, but I can't allow you to get tangled in my affairs. I respect you too much for that. This is my battle, not yours."

"It's mine now. When justice no longer prevails, a man has to do what he must do in order to put matters right. I believe I can count on Colonel Bates's help. We could use diversion tactics if necessary, and if the elements cooperate, we should be able to pull it off without a hitch."

"Can Colonel Bates be trusted, Sir?"

"It's true that Colonel Bates is volatile at times, but he can be trusted. You have my word on that. Let me work out the details; meanwhile, forget we had this conversation."

"I will, Sir, I will...but I don't know how to repay you for all your kindness."

"I would be less than a man if I did not wash your feet, and I have no doubt you would deal with me accordingly, if the occasion arose."

"No doubt, Sir."

They shook hands and parted.

Judge Selassie was a most unusual man.

Chapter 9

The malarial season was nearing, and the evening before the Charity Ball, Victoria fell ill with a fever. Judge Selassie called in a doctor from Charleston. Colonel Bates got wind of it and accompanied the doctor to the Selassie plantation; he was frightfully worried about his beloved Victoria, and hoped for an audience with her, but she refused to see him.

To everyone's relief, it proved to be only a nasty summer cold, but Victoria would not be attending the ball. "Oh do leave me be, all of you, before I am completely overcome with self-pity," Victoria scolded. "I want nothing more than for Mandy to shut out the light in my room, for I am totally languishing for sleep."

Satisfied that this was the case, the doctor prescribed bed rest and a tonic of sorts.

After the doctor left, Walter Selassie joined Colonel Bates and Tray Hampton in the study. York guessed they were talking "man-talk" while quenching their thirsts on Mandy's mint iced tea. She picked up her book of verse and retreated to the rose garden.

The roses had never been so pretty and the euphonious singing of the birds always lifted her spirits. She sat motionless throughout their performance, savoring every note. She knew how much Victoria was looking forward to the annual charity ball and not being able to attend was a grave disappointment for her. She would pick a bouquet of flowers for her in the cool of the evening...roses always smelled sweeter at dusk or early in the morning.

Mr. Clark, the low country pony express rider, came to deliver the mail. York walked out to meet him. She exchanged courtesies with him and he proceeded to tease her. "Now let me see...no, I don't see anything addressed to a Miss York Selassie here. Maybe it got lost somewhere along the way." The disappointment was registered on York's face and Mr. Clark didn't have the heart to prolong her agony. "Wait a minute, I do believe there is a small post here — why yes, here it is! He held it up to the light. There's no return address on it...hmm, now I wonder who that could be from?"

"Mr. Clark, you are such a tease! I know very well that you know almost everything about everybody on your route."

He laughed good-heartedly and waved off. "Give my regards to the Judge."

"I will, Sir. Thank you."

York hugged the letter close to her breast, and returned to her "alcove of serenity" in the rose garden. She hurriedly tore open the envelope.

Dear York,

God only knows where I am now. There is a rumor going around the camp that the Union Army under General McDowell is advancing toward Manassas Junction, Virginia. There is a strong possibility our regiment will be called up as reinforcements for our troops stationed there. That's about all I know about the war.

By the time we made camp tonight, I had worn blisters on both my feet. My companions keep reminding me that I am wearing "Yankee" boots. I had traded coffee and tobacco rations for them, considering I had no need for either. Yankee boots or not, I am grateful for them in this rough terrain. We marched through several towns and villages today. The folks in Virginia have welcomed us with open arms. Occasionally we are invited into private homes for a warm meal, but it's the nights I dread the most. That's when boredom sets in. I miss you. Some of the soldiers play cards, others sing around the campfire, and a few find a quiet corner and read their Bibles.

The light is fading. I must close. Remember me with fondness.

Andrew Foy

~ ~ ~ ~ ~

"Boom!" "Boom!" "Ba-ro-o-m!"

York jumped. The cannon volleys sent chills coursing throughout her body and her book and letter sliding to the garden walk. Even more startling was Tray Hampton's voice. "It's only target practice, Miss York. I have observed that it occurs around this time every morning." He stooped to retrieve her belongings. He noted Andrew Foy's signature, and a frown creased his brow.

"Mr. Hampton, Sir, I didn't hear your footsteps."

"I'm glad you didn't, Miss York, else you would have slipped away before I had emblazoned this vision of loveliness on the canvas of my mind. I must say your sister, Victoria, is a lovely painting, but you, Miss York, are a masterpiece."

"And what would you know about a masterpiece, Mr. Hampton, or for that matter, what lies beneath the surface?"

"Oh, my lady, I know many things about you — you are a romantic, of a sprightly disposition, tempered by refinement, and you cannot abide Tray Hampton."

"How you do go on, Mr. Hampton. It so happens that I am trying desperately to understand Shakespeare. Tell me, do you read much?"

"Some."

"Then, read to me, Sir. Read it the way it is supposed to be read."

"I will try, Miss York. May I sit beside you?"

York reluctantly moved to the far end of the bench. Tray pretended not to notice. How noble she sat among the flowers, the most beautiful flower of all. His heart was beating fast; if only he could reveal its rhythm. York was not like other women — with York it would take time.

"You do know how to read, don't you, Mr. Hampton?"

His presence was quite discomfiting. She was remembering things a lady should not remember...the closeness of him on the Ashley River Road, the vacancy in the hollow of her stomach...his blue-gray eyes steeled on hers.... But she must not remember, for Victoria was pining away for him and refusing to be comforted.

And does he care? How little she knew him.

41

Tray read Sonnet XXIV:

> *"Mine eye hath play'd the painter and hath stell 'd...*
> *Thy beauty's form in table of my heart;*
> *My body is the frame wherein 'tis held,*
> *And perspective it is best painter's art,*
> *For through the painter must you see his skill,*
> *To find where your true image pictur'd lies,*
> *Which in my bosom's shop is hanging still,*
> *That hath his windows glazed with thine eyes,*
> *Now see what good turns eyes for eyes have done;*
> *Mine eyes have drawn thy shape, and thine for me*
> *Are windows to my breast, where-through the sun*
> *Delights to peep, to gaze therein on thee;*
> *Yet eyes this cunning want to grace their art,*
> *They draw but what they see, know not the heart..."*

York was deeply moved. For the first time, *The Sonnets* had come alive for her. Aunt Penelope was right...Mr. Hampton is indeed a master of articulation.

"Shall I go on, Miss York?"

"What?"

"I said, shall I — you haven't heard a word I've read, Miss York."

"I beg your pardon, Mr. Hampton, I heard every word. That was...quite nice, but I must go now. Perhaps another time..."

"Why must you always run from me, Miss York?"

She turned away and toyed with the pink ribbons of her bodice, not knowing quite how to answer him.

"Remember what I told you on the Ashley River Road? One must never turn one's back upon the enemy?"

This struck a responsive cord in her. She laughed, drawing out his laughter. "I remember how I rendered you foolish that day."

"Not half as foolish as you will look when I turn you over my knee and spank you, my lady."

"You wouldn't dare!"

"Oh, wouldn't I?"

Tray lunged for her. York darted out of his reach and ran straight into the arms of her father, who happened to be coming

out the door of the Manor House with Colonel Bates at this pre-
cise moment. Tray, following her in hot pursuit, stopped abruptly.

"Hear, hear, Mr. Hampton," her father scolded, "this is not the
way we treat our women in the South!"

"Sir, I...I..."

"It's all right, Father, it was my fault." York explained, "We
were just evening up an old score."

"Is that true, Mr. Hampton?"

"Yes, Sir!"

"Well...who won?"

"She did, Sir."

Chapter 10

The blonde, wide-eyed Victoria recovered from her illness, looking pale but more beautiful than ever. Not having a proper suitor at hand, she prevailed upon Tray Hampton to drive her around the countryside in her Father's open carriage. She was convinced that the fresh air would do her more good than all the doctors in Charleston.

"York, dear," she said in Tray Hampton's presence, "there is nothing I would like more than for you to ride with us, but Father insists that you resume your studies with Mrs. Comstalk." Victoria was only two years York's senior and the difference in their ages qualified her to be the mistress of the plantation — albeit, a self-appointed one.

"Of course," she agreed, "I certainly would not want to lose favor with Father, or Mrs. Comstalk for that matter."

Tray Hampton smiled and bowed slightly from the waist in his usual manner. "You shall be greatly missed, Miss York."

"I'm satisfied I will not be missed at all, Mr. Hampton. Have a pleasant drive, both of you." She noted that he was not altogether displeased with the prospect of squiring Victoria around the countryside. After all, Victoria was the belle of Charleston society, and men naturally gravitated toward her. She almost envied Victoria's enchanting beauty, but envy was nothing more than jealousy running amuck. She checked her emotions and mustered the courage to face Mrs. Comstalk.

York fully expected the worst. Mrs. Comstalk was hawk-like and focused, zeroing in on her prey. "How nice to see you, York. Do come in. No, don't sit there. Come over here and let me have a look at you. My, how pretty you are — a fashionable lady after the style of the paintings of Winterhalter."

Mrs. Comstalk was a swan! She was in a jovial mood today. York had never seen this side of her before. "Godey's Lady's Book, as interpreted in the East, so I'm told," York shyly replied. "I rather prefer a more simple form of dress."

"Yes, the all-pervasive conventionality of clothing is debatable. It's surprising how much importance we place upon the latest fashions here in the South when there is a war going on."

"I couldn't agree with you more."

"I received a bittersweet letter from Mr. Comstalk today."

"I trust he is well?"

"Yes, yes indeed, and a reconciliation between us may soon be resolute."

"That's wonderful, Mrs. Comstalk."

"Yes, that's the sweet part. The bitter part is that he is in a very vulnerable position working on our railways, and I am gravely concerned for his safety; however, he tells me not to worry, for President Jefferson Davis has vowed that our Confederate railways will be defended at all cost. I fear I have treated him abominably — but dear York, I simply could not control his taste for the 'devil's brew,' as you well know. He assures me he has repented of all his past deeds and I suppose I love him enough to believe it. Today my joy knows no bounds!"

"I'm glad you shared this moment with me, Mrs. Comstalk." It made York feel older and somewhat her equal. "I admire your magnanimity."

"I can be generous in forgiveness now, but tomorrow I may fail him. Tell me, York, do you believe education is only for the young?"

"Oh no, it's never too late to learn."

"I'm glad you feel that way, for there are some things you need to know." Mrs. Comstalk was focused now.

"I...I'm sorry I have been avoiding my studies...but..."

"Poppycock! I have taught you more than most girls know already."

Was this her tutor, Mrs. Comstalk, speaking?

"I do not wish to alarm you, but these are troublesome times and today you are going to begin to receive a *real* education. Have you ever picked, carded, dyed, and spun your own thread into cloth?"

"Why no, neither has Victoria."

"Have you ever gathered medicinal herbs, dried them, dipped candles, or made your own soap with lard and ashes?"

"I wouldn't know how."

"Do you know how to dress a hen or milk a cow?"

"I'm afraid not. Mandy won't let me come near the kitchen unless it is to set the table. Paddy and Aaron milk the cows, but I do help Victoria dress the rose garden. Then there is my reading, needlework, and music; and Aaron has taught me how to ride and saddle Duchess."

"That is good, but there is so much more you need to learn. We will begin today...." And begin they did!

Little did York realize at the time how valuable those lessons would be in the days and months ahead.

~ ~ ~ ~ ~

When Victoria returned from her outing with Tray Hampton, York noticed the bloom on her cheeks. Victoria was flushed and excited; she talked about what a lovely time they had. "It was such a beautiful drive and Mr. Hampton was most attentive to my person."

"I have no doubt of it, Victoria."

"Have you noticed his deep blue-gray eyes, how penetrating, how intelligent?"

She had.

"Oh silly me, here I am prattling about Mr. Hampton, and I haven't asked you about your day."

York knew Victoria was not really interested in how she passed the day, but she would humor her. "I milked a cow today."

Victoria was no more surprised at York's reply, than was York, when she saw the look on Victoria's face.

Chapter 11

Tray Hampton's thoughts were legion. If he was going to run the blockade, he would have to do it before hurricane season. His departure would not be immediate, but imminent. At any given moment he would be "crossing the Rubicon."

He had staged it all in his mind and played the part of the protagonist (a Confederate Captain) over and over again. The real Shipmaster and the crew would be waiting in the wings. They would row out to the ship under a dense fog with padded oars and provisions for their journey, praying all the while they would not be detected by the lookout boats stationed in the harbor at night. They would then hover in the shadow of the big ship and wait for the proper signal to board.

Meanwhile, he, along with the Shipwright, with the ship's papers in hand (though falsified) would approach the pickets. Orders would be given to repair the ship — repairs that were not necessary, but which would afford the Shipmaster and his crew some sorely needed time. If he was questioned, he was to say that the Confederate Navy had need of the ship, and if in doubt, the picket would be prompted to telegraph the proper authorities. Colonel Bates would be on the other end of the line.

Tray Hampton and his accomplices would ease out of the channel, and after they passed Ft. Moultrie, Sullivan's Island, and Morris's Island, they would head out to sea at breakneck speed. Ship-rigged and with halyards in hand, they would then lower the

Confederate flag, raise the British flag, and sail on to Boston under the guise of Her Majesty's ship.

Perchance the fog should not lift until morning, and they had cleared the bay area undetected, they would then sit quietly in open waters until they could effect their escape. Hopefully, they would be out of the range of the big cannons, for when morning came they would surely be spotted and fired upon when their plot was discovered.

There would be no good-byes. Not even the Judge would know the exact time of the departure even though he was the one who had fostered the well-laid plans. Tray had insisted that Judge Selassie must not in any way expose his family to undue harm. If their deed was discovered, there would be a bounty on *both* their heads and most assuredly a hanging or firing squad in due process of time. Tray prayed that God would be at the helm of the ship, else all would be for naught.

When the curtain of sleep was drawn, Tray dreamed of York, only to awaken to reality. She had scorned his affections upon every meeting. He loved everything about her — her saucy demeanor and ready wit, her keenness of mind, and childlike innocence — even her proud chin held high. He couldn't help but compare her with Victoria. If Victoria was the essence of womanhood, York was the flowerage of it. She was someone with whom he would like to grow old, and love and cherish all the days of his life. How ironic, he thought; Victoria seemingly favored him, but it was York's name he had engraved upon his heart. Her face was always before him. He would look for an opportune time to be alone with her before he stealthily slipped away, and he vowed to return one day, despite the danger he might face. To never see York again was unthinkable!

When dawn broke, a peace came over Tray, along with the promise of blue skies and a golden day in the sun. It was his usual habit to go walking early in the morning before breakfasting with the Selassie family and the Rector. He had not yet figured out what role the Rector played in the drama of life, for he was not like any other clergyman Tray had ever known. He appeared to be financially substantial; and one thing was certain, he liked Mandy's cooking.

Tray thought he heard a stirring in the hay near the carriage house. Perhaps it was only the shuffling of horses' hooves in the stables nearby. He heard it again, but this time there was laughter. He rounded the corner and saw Aaron sporting with a pretty young mulatto girl. He released her hurriedly and shielded her behind his back.

"Mr. Hampton, Sir, this is my girl, Miss Sudie Mae Brown. Sudie Mae keeps house for the Rector. She rode in with him this morning. We are going to be married."

"Why hello, Miss Sudie Mae Brown." Sudie Mae peeped out from behind the broad-shouldered Aaron, and smiled. She had a nice row of even white teeth.

"You won't tell the Judge you saw us will you, Sir?"

"You mean the Judge doesn't know?"

"No, Sir. He has never even met Sudie Mae. I was going to tell him as soon as we had made our wedding plans."

"Your secret is safe with me, Aaron, but I wouldn't wait too long to get married if I were you."

"Yes Sir, Mr. Hampton, I'm much obliged to you, Sir."

"You're welcome."

"Yes Sir, thank you, Sir."

Aaron was a well-mannered person. His speech was quite good — unlike the Gullah language that most black Charlestonians spoke. Tray wagered that Walter Selassie had tutored him in writing as well. Life was not easy for the black folks. He firmly believed that, given the opportunity, Aaron could make his mark in the world.

"I'll be on my way now, Aaron. I see the Rector's horse is tethered at the hitching post. He must have gotten up earlier than I did, this morning."

"His horse threw a shoe, Sir. I replaced it."

"That was kind of you, Aaron."

"Good day, Miss Brown. I congratulate you both." Sudie Mae fairly beamed and Aaron's chest swelled with pride. At that moment, Tray envied their newly found happiness.

~ ~ ~ ~ ~

Tray found Walter Selassie and the Rector in jovial moods. The women folks were stirring around like field mice, and he could hear their soft chatter coming from the direction of the kitchen.

"Mr. Hampton, Sir," the Rector said in a sonorous manner, "We were just speaking of you — I hear you're interested in studying Law. Get you a somber black suit, white linen shirt, a tall silk hat and gaiters, like Walter here, and you would exemplify the lawyer-statesman. Who knows, you might become another Abraham Lincoln."

The Rector's jesting puzzled Tray. It was hard to tell where his loyalties lay. Was he trying to pour salt into the Judge's wounds, considering his decision to quit the South? But of course, the Rector would not be privy to this information unless the Judge had chosen to confide in him.

"Well, Rector, if I were saddled with a name like Jonas, I believe I would at least try to live up to it," Walter Selassie replied. "Who knows, the Lord just might reproduce Himself through you. Now let's eat, folks, before the Rector decides to test one of his new sermons on us."

Tray surmised that this must be some private joke between them.

Chapter 12

The opportune time for Tray to approach York came the following weekend.

Colonel Bates arrived early on Saturday morning and drove Victoria into Charleston to view the three o'clock dress parade at the Citadel. Afterward, they would be dining at the Mills House. Victoria would be staying overnight with friends and returning the following morning. Mrs. Comstalk was keeping company with York, while Mandy, Paddy, and Aaron were supervising the household chores in Walter Selassie's absence.

Tray talked Mandy into preparing a picnic basket in hopes that York would accompany him on an outing down by the riverside. He knew it wasn't good enough for her, but his subsistence in his present crisis was meager, for the South Carolina authorities had forbade the United States Sub-Treasurer of Charleston to cash any more drafts from Washington.

To Tray's surprise, York accepted his invitation, providing he would assist her in collecting and cataloging medicinal herbs for Mrs. Comstalk. Strolling through the meadow with their baskets in hand, Tray confessed that he knew absolutely nothing about medicinal or culinary herbs.

"Neither do I, Mr. Hampton, but I must say this is more fun than being cloistered in a dark room all day with Mrs. Comstalk. She never opens her curtains to let the sunshine in — she says the

53

glare bothers her eyes. With Mr. Comstalk away, I believe she is lonely and depressed most of the time."

"I had an idea you might be looking for an escape, else how could I have gotten you to come with me?"

"I have a confession to make also, Mr. Hampton, I brought my book of verse along. Do you suppose a digression from collecting herbs could be the order of the day?"

"Ah, a true Renaissance woman. I will tell Mrs. Comstalk that the spirit was willing, but the flesh was weak."

There it was again — York's contagious laughter. The wind ruffled her dress and a chill went over her. Tray noticed she had set her basket down and was hugging her arms. He noticed everything about her...the way her chestnut hair caught the sunlight, her dimpled cheeks all aglow, and soft pink lips, full and curled just right at the corners. She was wearing yellow with a black velvet ribbon accentuating her petite waist. As they strolled through the meadow, butterflies fluttered over the folds of her dress and followed in her wake. Surely this must be an apparition, he thought.

The fallen leaves along the Ashley River were curling and rouged in russet. A strong wind was blowing in from the east. Tray draped his coat around York's shoulders and freed her hair from beneath the collar. He would have kissed her proud, patrician neck, right then and there, but he thought better of it. Meanwhile, he would redeem the remaining time he had to spend with her.

"Have you recently heard from your young man, Mr. Foy?"

"Please, Mr. Hampton, do not refer to him as *my* young man. Mr. Foy is a dear friend, that is all."

"Forgive me if I have offended you, Miss York. Your sister led me to believe that Mr. Foy had sought your hand in marriage."

"Then you must have been grossly misinformed, Mr. Hampton, Sir. It has been some time since we have corresponded. Andrew fully expected his regiment to be called up to reinforce our Confederate forces in Manassas Junction. I have no idea when I shall see him again."

"I'm sorry." Even as he said this, he knew he was not sorry, but encouraged.

"Yes," she agreed. "I can't imagine gentle Andrew bearing arms against his brothers. I fear this is going to be a protracted war. Father said he is already beginning to see some shortages in the market places, and Mrs. Comstalk believes perilous days are ahead."

"Yes. Power and greed have devoured many a civilization."

"If you are referring to slavery here in the South, Mr. Hampton, we have never owned a slave. Father pays the Lewis family well for their services."

"Slavery comes in many forms, Miss York. We must all act responsibly."

"I agree with you Sir, but do our lawmakers act responsibly by allowing slavery in some states and forbidding it in others? Do we act responsibly by allowing the wealthy citizen (for a certain fee) to exercise exemption from war, when the common man is conscripted into service?"

Tray did not quite know how to answer her. He would change the subject. "Miss York, I perceive that you are very astute. Shall we spread our lunch now?"

"We shall indeed. I am simply famished."

Tray spread a cloth on the ground and drew two sandwiches and a pair of pewter cups out of his picnic basket. Mandy had thought of everything. He plucked wildflowers from the meadow and set them in a tin of water. York watched him in amusement. They sat beneath the "old man with a beard," and ate their lunch. Tray inquired about the relationship between Victoria and Colonel Bates.

"Colonel Bates has been courting Victoria for some time and he is totally smitten with her. As for Victoria, the feeling may, or may not, be mutual. I really couldn't say."

York grew pensive. Victoria was fickle. She knew Victoria held Colonel Bates on a tight leash, and she would not readily give him up. She suspected Mr. Hampton had an ulterior motive for inquiring about their relationship and perhaps that's why he had pressed her into joining him today. There were laconic moments when York dared to believe that Mr. Hampton really enjoyed *her* company. He was a philanderer! She quietly reprimanded herself...she was such a simpleton. She, like Victoria, had almost succumbed to his charms.

Tray arose from where he was seated. "Miss York, I can't offer you chamber music, but would you dance with me?"

"I beg your pardon, Sir?"

"May I have this dance with you?" Tray's movements were slow and decisive — the click of the heels and the bow.

"Mr. Hampton, Sir, I..."

"Are you afraid of me?"

"Really, Mr. Hampton you are incorrigible! But just to show you that I'm not afraid, I will dance with you."

Tray's hand gently encircled York's waist. She straightened. His right hand clasped hers, hiding it in his. His steps were not awkward, but smooth and deliberate. They danced to the music of the wind and the rustling of the leaves. York soon became pliant in his arms as they circled the ballroom of the great outdoors. Tray sensed the change in her demeanor, but she protested when he tried to draw her closer to him; howbeit, this was a moment in time he would take with him and cherish no matter what happened.

The shadow of the blockade faded into nonentity. There were just the two of them, each lost in their own reverie, content for a season. Tray knew York did not love him, but he would win her love, for he had purposed in his heart to marry her.

"Miss Selassie," he whispered in her ear, "One day I will marry you and ride the dappled mare."

"Mr. Hampton, Sir," she softly scolded, "I will never marry you, and you will never ride my dappled mare."

Chapter 13

It was a quiet evening in Charleston's harbor. The fog moved in stealthily and a ghostly fleet of ships appeared to ring the bay area. On nights like these, the pickets were prone to fire at anything within earshot, be it man or apparition.

To Tray Hampton's relief, not one shot was fired as he and the crew effected their escape. The only problem was the fog. Wasn't this what he had hoped for — even prayed for? Visibility grew steadily worse, and the captain and crew could not find their way out of the bay area.

It looked as if the mission would have to be aborted, when suddenly out of the mist, a tugboat flashed her signal light, and her Pilot persuaded the Shipmaster and crew to follow in her wake as she guided them to the mouth of the harbor. Was this part of the plan?

With full confidence in his Shipmaster, Tray stood and watched as the broad figure of a man, wearing a dark cape, slowly maneuvered the small tugboat into the shadow of their ship to lead them seaward. Tray could scarcely make out the name on her bow in the haze, but the Shipmaster recognized the boat as *The Angel of Mercy*. The little tugboat and its Pilot didn't leave off until the *Parvenu* was guided safely over the bar and out of harm's way.

To Tray Hampton's surprise, he learned that the tugboat captain was none other than the Rector himself, flying a red hospital banner!

~ ~ ~ ~ ~

The next morning at the Selassie Plantation, two chairs at the breakfast table were noticeably vacant — Tray Hampton's and the Rector's. Mandy came rushing in with plates of food piled high; little did they know the Rector was suffering from a very bad cold.

"Mistah Walt, it sho' is quiet in heah' dis' mornin' — like as how deres' a wake a'goin' on by de' looks on all yo' faces. Where all de' men folks be dis' mornin'? I's done gone an' fixed de' preacher and Mistah Hampton a special treat."

"I would guess Mr. Hampton is sleeping in this morning, but I can't figure out why the Rector hasn't arrived yet. Mandy, ask Aaron to take a tray up to Mr. Hampton and inquire about his well being."

"Yes 'suh."

Victoria voiced her disappointment. "Well, I for one, consider Mr. Hampton's absence a personal affront to the family."

"I understand perfectly," Mrs. Comstalk quipped. "Women, in general, learn by precept upon precept, while men are less thoughtful when it comes to matters they perceive to be trivialities."

"I see right now that I am outnumbered, ladies," the Judge replied. "Please excuse me for interrupting this diatribe against the male population, but let's consider Mr. Hampton the exception, if you don't mind."

Walter Selassie had a pretty good idea why Tray was not at the breakfast table that morning, and right now he was gravely concerned for his safety. He would not rest until word came to him that Tray had successfully crossed the bar into the Bay of Boston.

~ ~ ~ ~

Later in the day, when Tray was absent for dinner at the usual hour, it started the household tongues to wagging again.

Walter knew that sooner or later he would have to take his daughters into his confidence. Meanwhile, he would fain surprise over Tray's departure and when the deed was exposed, he would try to convince everyone that Mr. Hampton was only a guest in his house, and that if it had not been for the ill treatment by the Confederacy, Tray would not have executed his escape and speeded his parting.

The *Charleston Mercury* reported that the *Parvenu,* an English ship, captured in the bay area, and prized for her cargo, had successfully escaped the blockade. The pickets were reprimanded and dismissed. A full investigation was to be undertaken and all parties involved in her escape would be tried for treason and punished in the most severe manner according to the laws of the State of South Carolina.

It had been an embarrassment to the Confederacy to say the least, not to mention the loss of profits to be gained by the respective privateers. And, how safe were Charleston's harbors? Charlestonians wanted to know.

Chapter 14

The Mayor and a few of the leading citizens of Charleston, boarded a flatboat and cruised down the Ashley River to pay a visit to Judge Selassie.

It was not unusual for distinguished guests such as Statesmen, Legislators, Generals, and Academicians to frequent the Manor House, as the Judge was noted for his ready wit, wisdom, and hospitality; however, this was not intended to be a social call, but an interrogation party in behest of the *Parvenu* incident. Jonas White, the Rector, got wind of the party and secretly informed the Judge, and even accompanied the party down river. If need be, he would vouchsafe the Judge's innocence.

Upon their arrival, the preparation for the noon meal was under way. The Judge prevailed upon the gentlemen to join him and his family for a sumptuous meal of wild duck and rice. Afterward there was music and singing in the parlor. The Selassie sisters were most charming — York playing the harp, and Victoria accompanying her on the flute. Mrs. Comstalk, seated at the piano, sang like a nightingale. The men joined in the singing and occasionally belted out a few bars of "God Save The South." The interrogation party was so enamored with the ladies they almost forgot their real mission.

The ladies excused themselves and the men folks retired to the library to smoke their pipes and wrangle over the escalation of the war. The afternoon grew long, and knowing that the party had a long trip up river before dark, the Judge inquired into the purpose of their visit. One of the elderly spokesmen cleared his throat nervously and, in an apologetic manner, broached the subject of the *Parvenu*.

"Perhaps you haven't read the *Charleston Mercury*, Walt, but the *Parvenu* escaped our pickets in the harbor and ran the blockade a fortnight ago."

"You don't say?" The Judge queried, feigning surprise. Unbeknownst to the others, the Rector winked over at the Judge and laid a finger aside his nose and snorted.

"Confound it, Walt," the mayor blurted out, "We need money to fight this war. That ship and its cargo would have meant a lot of money for our fair city."

And to line your own pockets, no doubt, Walter Selassie was thinking.

"That's not all, Walt," one of the citizens enjoined. "President Jefferson Davis has placed a ban on all cotton shipments going to England in hopes she will recognize the Confederacy as a valid nation. Now our cotton is rotting on the docks and we need our money."

"I see," the Judge agreed. "That doesn't seem prudent during a time of war."

"The North, South, and England, are all wanting to know the whereabouts of that ship and its cargo," the mayor complained. "You see, the *Parvenu* never made port in Boston or England."

Walter Selassie's brow furrowed. The words "never made port" tore at his heart. It must not be true...or else... He sucked in his chest and breathed deeply, cognizant of the dangerous position in which he had placed Tray Hampton.

"How can you be so sure the ship never made port?" he asked.

"Supposition is, the ship may have been pirated, or sank off the coast of England," a member of the party surmised.

The Judge collected himself, and tried not to jump to conclusions, given the fact that he had not heard any foreboding news from Hugh Hampton. Somehow, all this didn't pass the "smell" test.

"We're asking for your help, Walt," the spokesman added.

"This is an international matter, gentlemen. Who's to say I have jurisdiction?"

The party mumbled something about the Judge's political clout and influence abroad, and then proceeded to the topic of Hampton Freight Lines, and Tray Hampton, the Judge's recent house guest.

The Judge was not listening anymore. They had no proof of his involvement in the *Parvenu* case, and he was a Judge who couldn't be bought. Little did the interrogation party realize he had been forced to choose his colors; howbeit, blue looked better on him than gray. As a matter of fact, it was looking better every day!

Walter Selassie had done all he could to foster the escape of the *Parvenu*. He had warned Tray he would have no protection in open waters, but he took consolation in the fact that no storms had been reported at sea as yet. More than likely, Tray had anchored in some foreign port...but of course, piracy couldn't be ruled out! He wanted to send a wire to his friend, Hugh Hampton, but he suspected the telegraph lines were being monitored.

~ ~ ~ ~ ~

A few days later, after Walter Selassie had set his affairs in order, he decided to board a steamboat and cruise up north to glean any information he could find pertaining to the ship and crew. Somewhere along the way, he was caught in the crossfire between two opposing parties, one from the North and one from the South. A shot rang out! He felt the hot ball pierce his chest, and saw the crimson flow spilling over the deck. His whole life flashed before him. He reddened, paled, and then turned a ghostly gray. A warm light enveloped him...

~ ~ ~ ~ ~

Walter York Selassie was brought back to the low country and buried beside his beloved Abigail. For the remainder of the year of 1861, a black wreath hung on the door of the Manor House. The gloom that overtook the Selassie family could not be assuaged by friends who stopped by frequently to pay their condolences. That first winter, it seemed that the war was frozen in time, and hearts were stillborn. Gone was the laughter, the parties, singing, and gaiety.

"Oh, the war, this terrible war!" York decried.

In time, the visitors fell away one by one...even the Rector no longer came by. And many moons later when the story was told, Mandy and Paddy kept alive this tale: "When dere' is a shadow on de' moon, Mis' Abigail can be seen a-standin' on de balcony of de' big house just a-watchin' and a-waiting' for Mistah Walt to come ridin' up a-stirrin' de' dust to git to her."

Chapter 15

There was quite a bit of activity along the North and South Carolina seacoasts and several wooden Union ships were sunk while engaged in battle with the Confederate Ironclads; both sides learned early in the war that wooden ships were obsolete. The Federals were keeping up the bombardment of supply ships trying to enter the harbor, but a few blockade runners managed to slip in under the cover of darkness. The blockade runners were Charleston's only salvation when manpower and ammunition became scarce. There were also a number of hungry people in the city of Charleston, and if it were not for the generosity of the wealthy and the blockade runners, many people would have starved to death. Things didn't look too promising for the South. The port of New Orleans, the South's greatest seaport, had been taken. With regard to the war of the Mississippi, many southerners had placed their faith in General Lee's Army of Northern Virginia, but the South was outnumbered by General McClellan's Union forces.

York had put her faith in the only One who could bring peace to the North and South, the Almighty God! She feared that Victoria would have succumbed to a mental breakdown after their Father's death, had it not been for Colonel Bates. York felt as if she was little comfort to Victoria, seeing that her own heart was grieving, as well.

Colonel Bates approached Victoria again with an offer of marriage, and to everyone's surprise, she accepted. He talked about making their home in the city of Charleston, and he proposed to build a mansion on the waterfront for Victoria. She was delicate, and he felt that the city with its fresh ocean breezes, would be more suited to her constitution than the low swampland in the summertime. Seeing that Victoria was torn between their marriage, and leaving York and the plantation, he decided to postpone his plans until after the war. In the meantime, he would move to the Manor House in deference to Victoria's wishes.

York was happy for them, but she felt like an albatross around their necks. She knew things would never be the same again; perhaps she would write her Aunt Penelope and Cousin Clarissa to see if a visit would be in order.

Meanwhile, Colonel Bates and Victoria opted for a large wedding and honeymoon at the Mills House. It would be more practical, they reasoned, considering the bad roads in the low country, and the fact that most of their acquaintances lived within a short distance of Charleston.

Victoria grieved over not being able to find proper slippers for her wedding dress. There was a shortage of goods, and it was not likely that any shoes would be available in the near future, but Colonel Bates got wind of a secret shipment that had just arrived. He pushed and shoved his way through a crowd of Southern Belles shopping in a warehouse in downtown Charleston, and found a beautiful pair of white satin shoes.

It was the most lavish and "talked about" wedding that some folks had ever been privileged to attend.

~ ~ ~ ~ ~

After the port of New Orleans fell into the hands of the North, the city was crawling with Union soldiers.

Aunt Penelope and Cousin Clarissa wrote how it grieved them they had not been able to attend the wedding. Aunt Penelope said her slaves were rebelling, and her crops had not been laid by. She feared the worst; she thought she could make it through the winter, but cloth was hard to find in New Orleans, and with the blockade, she guessed she would have to bring out the old spinning wheel to make Clarissa's dresses and clothes for the slaves.

She supposed it didn't make much sense to worry about such things, considering young southern men were as scarce as hens' teeth. "There are plenty of Yankee soldiers around," she wrote, "if Clarissa was so inclined to lean in their direction." She pointed out that the southern girls treat the Yankee soldiers with utter contempt, and she pities them. She said the women, as well, were not careful where they threw their slop — so much for the *genteel* sex — war has brought out their animal natures! I try to treat the soldiers all alike, she continued. After all, they are only young men fighting a war they didn't ask for.

"Well, my dears," she wrote in conclusion, "I pray for you all daily, and I miss my poor brother, Walt, dearly. Until we meet again..."

York was saddened by Aunt Penelope's letter. She would not be going to New Orleans any time soon.

~ ~ ~ ~ ~

York suspected that Aaron and the mulatto girl would also be getting married on the heels of Victoria's wedding. It would be nice having someone around to help Mandy with the chores. Patching up one of the old outbuildings for Aaron and Sudie Mae had proved to be a welcome diversion for York that year. She and Victoria gave out of their abundance to furnish the house, and promised to do everything they could to make it comfortable and cheerful.

Colonel Bates was able to obtain bricks from an old building in downtown Charleston, and Aaron and Paddy built a wide fireplace and chinked it tightly with mortar. They whitewashed the house and Mandy hung curtains over the windows. They weren't certain, but when everything was ready for occupancy, they thought they saw a lump in Aaron's throat, and a tear fall from Sudie Mae's cheeks.

They were married by Jonas White, the Rector, in a private ceremony. There wasn't time for a honeymoon, for it was hog-killing time, and Aaron and Sudie Mae put their hands to the chore.

The Foys on the neighboring plantation came over and lent a hand. The men folks butchered the hogs, and the women cleaned and put up the meat. They boiled the skins in the deep fat and made cracklings. It looked like there was enough meat to feed the whole countryside, but Colonel Bates pointed out that it would only last during the coming winter.

After the hams were salted down, packed in barrels, and placed in the smokehouse, they all sat down and visited until late in the evening. The Foys bragged about the war and how their boy fought so bravely against the Yankees at the Battle of Bull Run. You would have thought that Andrew had won the battle single-handedly to hear Mrs. Foy describe it. York did not want to hear about the war. She excused herself and retired to her room earlier than usual.

She was restless. She longed for sleep, but sleep did not come. She was lonely, and she missed Andrew more than she realized. He was always present this time of the year, and joining in the fall festivities. She wondered if he was lying under the stars tonight thinking of home. Was he warm? Was he hungry? Would he be coming home soon?

Chapter 16

Victoria and Colonel Bates were seemingly happy, but the stress of running the plantation was beginning to take its toll. Mandy fussed over the meals, complaining that she hardly had enough flour to put a meal together. Occasionally, Colonel Bates was able to buy goods confiscated by blockade runners, but these times were few and far between. So far, they had plenty of rice and beans and sometimes he traded those for other commodities. They needed supplies for their guests, and it seemed as if there were more visitors than usual that winter.

Mrs. Comstalk became a permanent boarder at the Manor House. Mr. Comstalk managed to come around more often, despite the war, and he served as an escort for the ladies when Colonel Bates was not around; however, York and Victoria rarely had time to leave the plantation.

The noose was drawing tighter and tighter around the neck of the South. If the South needed the war as a catharsis, they were now having second thoughts. No one had expected the conflict to last this long. Not only were they being choked off from the rest of the world, but there sprang up another menace — Partisan Rangers! They stalked the countryside stealing food, supplies, and horses.

One such ranger accosted York as she rode up to the barn after her morning ride. As she started to unsaddle Duchess, he growled, "Leave her be!" The stranger was quite disheveled and covered with sweat and grime. He had ridden his horse hard and fast. He remarked caustically, "I'll take that horse if you don't mind, and I'll take other liberties as well if you scream for help."

York was terrified of this vile creature. She saw he had already tied her late father's geldings to his saddle and now he wanted Duchess! Where was Aaron — or Paddy? She steeled herself at the thought of losing Duchess, but then she remembered the whip (a cat-o-nine-tails) hanging near Duchess's stall. She moved slowly backward, edging her way closer to the wall.

"That's right, li'l lady, move away from that horse."

York smiled and in a lilting voice, replied, "Sir, I don't know who you are, but nothing is too sacred for our brave men in uniform. If you will dismount, I will fetch you a drink of water from the pump and water your horse as well."

"Now you're a-talkin', li'l lady."

She had charmed him right out of his saddle.

Suddenly he felt the sting of a whip cut a swath across his back — then another — and another — and another! Duchess neighed loudly, and the scalawag fell in the dirt, yelling and writhing in pain.

If Colonel Bates and Aaron had not come riding up and heard the commotion, the ranger would have been a dead man for sure. It took both he and Aaron to pull York off of him. The Colonel threw the bleeding man over his horse and told him in no uncertain terms that if he showed his ugly face around the plantation again, he would be hung and quartered! The Colonel's temper was of such a nature the ranger was inclined to believe him. He slumped in his saddle and rode away like a scared fox with a pack of hounds on his heels. One thing was certain, they were never bothered by his ilk again! But even so, Colonel Bates vowed he would teach York how to use a rifle.

~ ~ ~ ~ ~

One winter evening a regiment of soldiers passed through the low country and asked for permission to camp overnight on the Manor House grounds. They were wearing such odds and ends of clothing that one could hardly identify them as Confederate soldiers. York and Mrs. Comstalk supplied them with scarves, gloves, and blankets, which had been donated by the Ladies' Aide Society. They had knitted some of these articles themselves and wrapped numerous cloths into bandages. York had even collected urine for the Society, only to learn later that it would be used for making bullets. Mrs. Comstalk said they needed the nitrate it contained for ammunition — "everyone knows you can't make bullets without nitrate," she said. York detested this task but realized there was no room for pride with a war going on around them.

Colonel Bates, Mandy, and Paddy served the soldiers a warm meal of flapjacks with molasses syrup, and Aaron fed their horses. York listened on into the night to the patriotic songs of the recruits as their voices wafted over the breeze and through her bedroom window. Someone was playing a French harp…it was a melancholy tune…

Chapter 17

Colonel Bates lost his storekeeper's position because of a fire that spread throughout the arsenal. Was the fire set deliberately or was it accidental? No one would ever know for sure. His was a precarious position at best. He had held this post long before the war began, but his sympathies were now with the South, so he had resigned his commission with the Union.

He considered joining the Confederacy, but his beloved Victoria's tears dissuaded him — and he wasn't getting any younger. He guessed he would hold out as long as he could. He would eke out a living on the plantation, but only until after the war. It would take most of his savings to pay the taxes and keep the place up, but he would do the best he could. All in all, he considered himself to be a lucky man.

~ ~ ~ ~ ~

"Mistah Bates! Mistah Bates!" Paddy cried out.

"What's wrong, Paddy?"

"Come quickly Suh'. Dat' Mr. Hampton, he be's back."

"Tray Hampton?"

"Dat's the one. I figger' I's a seein' a ghost, but it be's him, sho' nuff. He snuck up to de' carriage house and tole me not to tell anyone 'cept you and my Missus."

Colonel Bates was piqued. If someone was on Mr. Hampton's trail, the whole family could be in jeopardy.

Upon seeing the Colonel, Mandy cried, "Oh Mistah Bates, Mr. Hampton, he not know about Mistah Walt's death. He be's powerfully shaken, Suh."

Tray was holding his head in his hands, and when he looked up, the Colonel thought he saw a tear on his cheek and his lower lip quiver.

"Leave us alone, Mandy, Paddy. I will handle this."

Tray stood and courageously faced the Colonel.

"Mr. Hampton, you fool!" he barked, "Don't you realize there is a bounty on your head? If the Confederates find you here, they will hang you for sure!"

"I am well aware of that, Colonel."

"What makes you think I won't turn you in?"

"Because Judge Selassie said you were a man who could be trusted, Sir."

Colonel Bates cleared his throat and his tone mellowed somewhat.

"Well, why have you come?"

"I came to warn him...but I don't suppose it matters much now...How did he die?"

"It was a horrible accident. It seems that two men on board the steamship, on which the Judge was a passenger, got into an argument. They squared off with one another and Judge Selassie was caught in the crossfire. It's been very hard on the Selassie girls. Victoria and I were married in early March."

"I congratulate you, Sir."

"Thank you."

"And what of York, is she well?"

"Yes, she is here with us." Tray wanted to hear more, but this was not the time or place.

"You said something about warning the Judge. What's that all about?"

"I came to warn him that there was a 'Judas' in his midst. I felt that his life was in grave danger."

"A Judas?"

"Colonel Bates, Sir, I don't know exactly what to make of this, but the night I ran the blockade, I glimpsed a broad-shouldered, heavy-set man piloting a small craft. I didn't think much of it at the time until we reached open water. We were then intercepted by a larger vessel somewhere along the coastline. I perceived she was an English ship. A crew came on board the *Parvenu*, and seeing there was adequate room for more cargo, loaded forty barrels of flour into her hull. I was curious, so I opened one of the barrels to inspect them — there were guns, Colonel, and they were earmarked for Charleston. When I questioned them about this matter, I was told if I opened my mouth, I was a dead man. I took my chances, jumped overboard, and swam to shore. I couldn't go back to Charleston with a bounty on my head. The crew fired several rounds at me...would have killed me, too, had they not been such lousy shots. I suppose one man overboard didn't mean much to them, so they turned, and sped away right before my eyes, but not before I noticed one thing — a small craft following in her wake and flying a red hospital banner!"

"The Rector!" Colonel Bates conjectured.

"That was my conclusion, also, Sir."

"Well, well, Jonas White, the Rector. How could I have been so stupid? That would explain his absence from the Manor House for long periods of time. Mr. Hampton, you have just solved a mystery that had haunted the Judge and me for some time now. I apologize for thinking you a fool."

"I'm not following you, Colonel."

The Colonel then explained that ever since the arms buildup, and even before the war, large shipments of guns had been stolen from the United States, England, and other countries as well. "These were not privateers, but an international piracy ring operating around the globe...clever," the Colonel opined. "Ships carrying wounded soldiers and flying a red hospital banner would be less suspect than most. They changed their *modus operandi* often," he explained, "so as not to come under suspicion. The Judge had been on their trail for years. This is bigger than both of us, Mr. Hampton. Of course, we will have to report our latest findings to the authorities, and I'll wager there will be a substantial reward for you, and perhaps a prominent position in the service of the United States Government."

"My only interest, Colonel, is to be done with this, and sail back to England to continue my studies in law."

"That's commendable of you, Mr. Hampton. But, now you must stay for dinner."

"No, Colonel. I regretfully decline your generous offer, for I must make haste under the cover of darkness. I don't know who might be lurking in the shadows."

"Then, so be it. I understand. I wish you Godspeed, my friend."

"Thank you, Colonel."

He thought the Colonel was a right, jolly good fellow once he had gotten to know him. Tray turned and mounted his horse, taking one long look at the big house, hoping to get a glimpse of York, but to no avail. He sighed, but just as he started to ride off, he noticed a cloud of dust in the distance. The Colonel had seen it, too. He practically dragged Tray off his horse and called for Mandy to hide him in the carriage house.

"Come wid' me, Mistah Hampton, Suh'. I knows jest' where to hide you!"

Paddy and Aaron picked up the nearest tools to give the appearance of normalcy, while the Colonel met the Confederates at the entrance of the big house. There were four of them — two officers and a duo of young recruits. The officers said not a word, and proceeded to search the Manor House.

Victoria and York remained calm, considering they knew nothing of what had just transpired between the Colonel and Tray Hampton. The young recruits searched the outbuildings, the barn, and alas — the carriage house. Presently, they emerged from the carriage house blushing profusely. The Colonel didn't know why they were so red around the gills, but the soldiers saluted the Colonel and hastily rode away. What or whom they were looking for they never did say.

"What scared them off, Mandy?" the Colonel asked.

"Well suh', I hid Mistah' Hampton in de wardrobe, and I sat right down on de necessary (chamber pot) like as how I'sa takin' kere' o' my business, and when them young'ins walks in I jus' screams, lifts my skirts, and half-way moons em' — Weren't nuttin' to it. Dat's the fust' time I's ever raised my skirts to protect a white man!"

Colonel Bates and Tray Hampton doubled over with laughter. The Colonel felt the danger had passed, so he insisted Tray stay the night. Tray declined, but upon everyone's insistence, he did stay for dinner. He *was* tired and hungry. While he shaved and fresh-ened up a bit, Mandy dusted off his frock coat and shined his boots. He couldn't do much about his clothes; his collar was frayed, and he hoped York wouldn't notice. His visit would be cut short, but he planned to come back after the war and claim York as his prize. Was this wishful thinking? He hoped not.

York was swathed in yards of white cotton and lace — soft, delicate, and innocent. The sides of her chestnut hair were pulled up and fastened at the crown of her head, accentuating her high cheekbones. Tray ached to bury his head in the long tresses cas-cading and bouncing down her back, as she moved gracefully around the room. She was older now and somewhat more reserved. There was a sadness about her that troubled him, yet he knew that buried beneath this veneer of sorrow, there was still that spark of vitality he loved so well.

Victoria and the Colonel appeared to be quite compatible, and Mr. and Mrs. Comstalk were getting on well. Only two chairs were empty — the Judge's and the Rector's. Mandy and Paddy doted over Aaron's mulatto wife, Sudie Mae. Tray wasn't sure, but she appeared to be with child. Mandy followed her around, keeping a close watch over her and giving her the lightest of chores.

Too soon, it was time for Tray to leave. He shook hands with Colonel Bates, kissed Victoria on the hand, hugged Mandy ginger-ly, and planted a kiss on York's forehead. Thankfully, she didn't shrink back!

Little did Tray know, but that kiss never left York's forehead. It was like the brush of an angel's wings...soft...gentle, like a moist droplet from a cool brook on her blushing brow.

She remembered their first meeting, the nearness of him, and their friendly banter. She thought he was a bit too cocky and for-ward...but how could she forget the inflection in his voice as he read to her in the rose garden, his blue-gray eyes all the while searching for her reaction. What had she been afraid of...his lofty appear-ance...his keenness of mind...his self confidence? What was it her Father had said? "Tray Hampton will make a fine barrister one day!"

"Oh Mr. Hampton," she sighed, "Would that I had just met you on the Ashley River Road!"

~ ~ ~ ~ ~

77

On the heels of Tray Hampton's visit, York walked through the garden looking for some portent of spring — a crocus, or a green bud pushing up from the ground. The wind was stirring in the trees, and she could hear the lapping of the waves on the Ashley River. It was refreshing to be in the great outdoors again. She heard a rustling in the bushes nearby, and a large hand closed over her mouth — it was Andrew!

"Andrew! You scared me half to death! What are you doing here?"

"Be quiet. I think I'm being followed."

He was quite jittery, and there was a glazed look in his eyes. "I had to see you York. I couldn't go back home."

"Andrew, you are acting so strangely."

"I have quit the army, York."

"Do you mean to tell me you are a deserter?"

"Yes."

"I don't understand you, Andrew."

"I thought this would make things right with us. Isn't this what you wanted?"

"No. Not like this. Oh Andrew, tell me it's not true. You must go back."

"You don't know how it is, York... the war...the bloodshed...the folly of it all." He saw the disappointment registered on her face.

"Don't hate me, York. I couldn't bear it."

"I don't hate you, Andrew."

"Let's go away together, York. I love you and I always will. I have thought of nothing else!"

He suddenly became overbearing and unrestrained. He grabbed her, pinning her arms behind her back and kissing her hard on the lips, drawing blood.

She was repulsed. She thought him mad! Struggling to free herself, she cried out that she didn't love him and she never would! His expression turned to anger and disbelief; he was at a loss for words. Releasing her, he stealthily ran and fled in the direction from whence he came.

York was visibly shaken as she confided to Victoria of Andrew's visit. She believed that the Confederate soldiers who searched the plantation the day before were probably looking for Andrew instead of Mr. Hampton.

"Well, I never," Victoria sympathized. "I just wish the Colonel had been there, he would have thrashed Andrew for good! I never thought of him as being a coward. Do you suppose he went back to his unit?"

"I don't know, but what did I ever do to make him think he could take such liberties with me? He was always so meek and shy."

"Yes...well...Colonel Bates tells me war sometimes changes a man. It's good you found out what Andrew's character is really like. Mr. and Mrs. Foy will be devastated."

"True. I guess this is not the first time I have misjudged someone's character."

"I suppose you are referring to Mr. Hampton. York, I do believe he is attracted to you."

"Oh how you do go on, Victoria. Mr. Hampton could not possibly care for me."

"I saw how he looked at you yesterday. I think I have seen it all along, but I didn't want to admit it — to you or myself. I was rather infatuated with him at first, and I had hoped he felt the same way about me. Apparently, he didn't. After Father's death, I realized how much I needed Colonel Bates. He has always been there for me. Oh, it's not the romance I had imagined, but he makes me happy, and I feel comfortable with him."

"Why are you telling me this, Victoria?"

"I am concerned about you. You should be thinking of marrying some nice young man like Mr. Hampton. You have been so morose and unhappy of late. Are you afraid of falling in love?"

"Am I that transparent?"

"I just think you would be happier, that's all." Victoria was the proverbial matchmaker.

"Perhaps I *am* afraid of falling in love. But don't you see? I am not like you, Victoria. I cherish my independence. Horseback riding, along with books, music, and art, have always been my muse."

"Your *muse* will not suffice as you grow older. It is not good for a woman to be alone. The Good Book says so."

"Oh, but when I fall in love, it must be with someone who will love me without reservation. It must be with someone who treats me with equanimity, has strength of character — is genteel, unassuming, and Christ-like."

"Aren't you the romantic? I seriously doubt that any man could live up to your scrutiny."

"I know I'm not beautiful like you, Victoria, and I don't pretend to know the wit and wiles of womanhood when it comes to attracting a mate. But if perchance there is someone out there in the pool of mankind who fits this description, and God wills it, he will find *me*. If not, then I suppose I will become an old spinster by choice."

Chapter 18

Folks in the low country began to settle down into their normal routines once again now that the initial shock of a full scale war with the North had lost its allure. A number of Confederate soldiers came back home to plant their crops in the spring, returned to fight again, and were shipped back home in pine boxes.

In order to stop commerce to the southern states, the Federals felt they had to take the ports, for ships were continuing to slip through the blockade. It was common knowledge that many states and countries (England not withstanding) were taking advantage of the war to line their own coffers. This was a typical British trader's toast:

> *Here's to the Confederates that grow the cotton,*
> *the Yanks that keep up the prices by blockade,*
> *the Limeys that pay the high prices for it —*
> *to all three and a long war.*

The only Confederate ports left open on the Atlantic Coast and the Gulf of Mexico were Charleston, Wilmington, and Norfolk.

Generals Johnston and Beauregard were on the offensive against General U. S. Grant's Union Army. They moved approximately forty-five thousand men to Corinth, Mississippi. Grant was camped only twenty-two miles northeast of Corinth at Shiloh

Church. Johnston's Army of the Mississippi attacked Grant's Federal camps, and it appeared as if the South had the advantage, but on the next day, the Federals held their line. The *Charleston Mercury* reported that the South was outnumbered, low on ammunition, and running out of food. Despite heavy casualties on both sides, the South retreated to Corinth with their wounded. The Federals were too fatigued to pursue them. The Battle of Shiloh was the bloodiest conflagration since the war began. The conflict had become a horse of two colors (blue and gray) each neighing for a fight; but, when the fight became full-blown, neither side wanted to ride the dappled mare.

York and Mrs. Comstalk were horrified at the reports of casualties and the death of General Johnston. Words like, "Hells Lane," "Hornets Nest," and "Bloody Pond," leaped out among the pages of the *Mercury*. They scanned the list of dead and wounded to see if there were any names they recognized. One name stood out — Edwin Sheppard.

"Oh my poor Edwin," Mrs. Comstalk cried out, "Look at this York. Edwin has been wounded and taken to Corinth!"

"Edwin?"

"Yes, my nephew, Edwin Sheppard. Oh silly me, you wouldn't know Edwin. He is a widower; his mother was Mr. Comstalk's sister. I must inform Mr. Comstalk at once."

"I am so sorry," York sympathized.

"Yes, Edwin is such a fine young man. I must inquire as to the nature of his injuries; perhaps he needs me. They are asking for volunteers to care for the wounded."

Mrs. Comstalk was a woman of action; she would go to Edwin's aid, and nurse him back to health.

"Would you like for me to go with you?" York yearned to leave the plantation, and she felt as if she could be of help.

"Oh my dear, I would love to have your company, but I fear that with the war going on, Colonel Bates would never agree to let you go to Corinth. It would be much too dangerous."

"I'm not afraid. I could help with the sick and wounded, and I need to get away from the plantation for a while. Talk to the Colonel, Mrs. Comstalk, I'm sure he will listen to you."

"You really do want to go, don't you."

"Oh yes, I would love nothing more than to be your traveling companion."

"Then we shall see, Dear, we shall see."

That was all York wanted to hear. She was satisfied her proposal would be successful in Mrs. Comstalk's hands. Being of age, she could defy the Colonel's wishes, but out of respect for him as her temporary caretaker, she would await his answer.

~ ~ ~ ~ ~

It took Mr. and Mrs. Comstalk both to convince Victoria and the Colonel that it was safe for York to make the circuitous route to Corinth. It was only when Mr. Comstalk pledged secure passage via the railways that the Colonel reluctantly agreed. If all went well, they would make a speedy return.

The train was filled to capacity. Confederate soldiers were being shuffled to and fro the battlefields. They were most courteous to York and Mrs. Comstalk, assisting with the baggage and proffering their seats. The train stopped only long enough at the stations for the passengers to refresh themselves and have a morsel of bread and tea.

When they arrived in Corinth, it seemed that every home and warehouse had been turned into a hospital ward. With help from the locals as to Edwin Sheppard's whereabouts, they were directed to a warehouse in the vicinity of the business district. Upon their arrival, they found that doctors were few in number, cots with wounded soldiers lined the room; and volunteers were working around the clock serving hot meals, changing bandages, and dispensing clean clothes and linens. Others were assisting the doctors and comforting those lingering in the shadow of death. York was not prepared for what she saw next — men with black faces, or no faces at all, soldiers with arms and legs dismembered, and vacant eyes staring back at her. Many were suffering from gangrene; others were in shock. York felt faint, but she put her handkerchief to her nose and followed Mrs. Comstalk and a nurse's aide to the back of the building, where they were told they would find Edwin Sheppard.

Edwin was seated on the end of a cot, with one leg in a cast and various bandages covering the greater part of his upper body.

"Oh my poor Edwin!" Mrs. Comstalk exclaimed.

Edwin looked up in surprise and broke out in a wide smile.

"Aunt Hattie? My, my, aren't you a sight for sore eyes."

"Oh Edwin, I was so worried about you. I had to come. Does it hurt badly?"

"Now, now," he comforted her, "I am doing just fine. It's not as bad as it appears. I caught a bullet from a Henry (that's a 16-shot breech-loading rifle). My wounds are only superficial, with the exception of my leg, but I fully expect to be up and running in a few weeks." Looking past Mrs. Comstalk's bulk, he saw York.

"Say, who is this charming lady hiding behind you?"

"This is Miss York Selassie, the daughter of the late Walter York Selassie, God rest his soul. She was nice enough to come along as my traveling companion."

"It is indeed a pleasure to meet you, Miss Selassie. I'm sorry I can't rise to the occasion. I hope you understand."

"Indeed I do, Mr. Sheppard."

Mr. Sheppard was an affable young man and York liked him immediately. His growth of beard belied his twenty-eight years. His hair was the color of wheat and curved neatly around his ears and sidelocks. He wasn't exactly handsome, but his features were well-defined and proportional. He reached for his sack coat and tried to make himself more presentable.

"I apologize for my appearance. I haven't had an opportunity to shave yet."

"You look just fine, Edwin. Now don't exert yourself on your old Aunt's account."

"I really am doing well, Aunt Hattie. Just look around you. I am one of the more fortunate ones. I will be returning to Savannah as soon as I am able to make the trip, but some of these men will never see their home place again."

Edwin deprecated the fact that he had to leave the battlefield. He couldn't explain it, but it didn't seem right that he should have been spared when so many of his fellow soldiers were left behind…

What do you think of your boys now, Mother,
Lying cold on the ground and torn asunder,

One wears gray, the other blue,
So young, so brave, so true,
Is the war worth it all, dear Mother,
I wonder?

~ ~ ~ ~ ~

Nothing York had ever read could have opened her eyes to the horrendous effects of the war, as had her visit to Corinth. There were twelve to fifteen-thousand Confederate men who had been in their prime, but now were dead, or battle-scarred for life, to say nothing of the Federal losses. She had to admit she had led a sheltered life; she wondered when it would all end. It behooved her to return to the plantation, for she knew Victoria needed her. She surmised that if the war were not over soon, the male population on the plantations would be depleted; it would only be a matter of time before the Colonel would join the Confederacy, and Victoria's tears would be of no avail.

Chapter 19

So much had happened since Judge Selassie's death. York thought about Jonas White, the Rector, and how often he had supped at their table in his robes of righteousness, all the while betraying her father and dealing in stolen goods for ill-gotten gain. Imagine hiding behind the cloak of the church and the law in such a fashion! She was appalled. The paper suspected the Rector was a "Copperhead," and a member of the Golden Circle, one of the secret societies that had sprung up during the war. It was a well-known fact that President Lincoln had declared war against all "Copperheads," labeling them traitors. To be sure, this scandal had caused quite a stir among the clergy in Charleston and the low country.

It would only be a matter of time before the Rector would reap what he had sown. Colonel Bates and Tray Hampton would be brought to Washington to testify during the trial, along with a number of other witnesses. Sudie Mae was the Rector's housekeeper for a few years. The Colonel had questioned her for any pertinent information she might have, but he could tell she was oblivious to any wrong doing. This trial would be a good experience for Tray Hampton, albeit, an unpleasant one. He was well into his second year of law school in England. And he was fully expecting to be exonerated of all wrongdoing in the *Parvenu* case. According to the news reports from Boston and England, he was being hailed as a great man of courage by the Secretary and Treasurer of the United States.

York realized how much she missed Mr. Hampton. She had to admit she had been flippant with him at times, but her wily behavior had always served her well as a safeguard against pretentious flirtations from the opposite sex. She supposed if Mr. Hampton seriously cared for her, as Victoria was prone to believe, he would have voiced his intentions to Colonel Bates. If she were honest with herself, she didn't know how she felt about Mr. Hampton. She could not deny her physical attraction for him, or the fact that they shared a fondness for literary pursuits, and his harmless jousting with her had been stimulating. But she still did not know him well, and it wasn't likely that they would meet again for a very long while.

~ ~ ~ ~ ~

In the summertime, plantation owners became more conversant, indulging in various activities: hunting, charity balls, picnics, and political debates. The Colonel was planning a fox hunt for neighboring plantation owners and a ball afterwards. He knew how much Victoria loved that sort of thing, and it would be a good diversion from the war. Like most southern plantation owners, he wanted to give the appearance of an abundance of wealth; therefore, he would set a lavish table even though times were hard. Fish and game were still plentiful on the plantation, and Mandy had a knack for seasoning and dressing up the plainest of victuals.

Victoria sprang into action and called Mandy, York, and Mrs. Comstalk to come upstairs to the sewing room to assist her with her wardrobe.

"I simply do not have a thing to wear," Victoria fretted, "and I must look my best."

"Nor I," York enjoined, "so I will probably wear the same dress I wore to your wedding."

"That will never do, York, everyone will notice." Victoria, like all the rest of the upper class, thought one should never wear the same dress twice to a wedding or a ball.

"Do you like this one, Mrs. Comstalk?" Victoria looked quite stunning in a beige brocade, but decided it would be much too droll.

"Dear, in my opinion, the guests will never notice your dress with that beautiful lavaliere and your flawless skin."

"Thank you for your vote of confidence. Nevertheless, I would like something cooler and more youthful. Mandy do you suppose you could remove the sleeves from my green dress and add fresh lace to the bodice?"

"Yess'um, if I has da' time, but da' cookin' comes first."

"Never mind, Mandy, I will make do. York, your pink dress would be nice; why don't you wear that one?"

"Whatever you wish, Victoria."

It mattered little to York what she wore. It was not likely she would meet anyone among the gentry who wasn't married or already engaged. She thought about all the work that was yet to be done: candles to dip, flowers to be arranged, party favors for the women, perfumed soaps, and potpourri toiletries for the overnight guests. Victoria was planning the menu and the selection of linens and tableware; Mrs. Comstalk would be in charge of the games and entertainment for the ladies; and of course, Mandy and Sudie Mae would be responsible for the food preparation. Roses were plentiful on the plantation, and Sudie Mae knew how to make delectable jelly and desserts from rose hips. The Foys on the neighboring plantation had proffered their slaves to help Aaron with parking the carriages and tethering the horses. The Colonel was pleased that everyone took to their tasks with enthusiasm. He took the liberty to invite Edwin Sheppard, for he learned from Mrs. Comstalk that he was back in Savannah, and the Colonel thought he would be a good dinner companion for some of the younger women. He also had several eligible young men from the Citadel lined up to dance with the ladies. He hoped he had not been remiss in seeing that everyone would have something enjoyable to do. After the three-day hunt and ball, there would be a lavish breakfast and sendoff on the weekend. He hoped the elements would cooperate, and the roads would not be muddy. Unbeknownst to Victoria, this party was a balm to soften the blow when he had to tell her he had received a letter from President Jefferson Davis calling for more Confederate troops. He felt as if he could not evade his duties any longer. It was not what he wished but he could not ignore the President's call to arms. He was advised that he could keep the position of rank he once held in the United States, if he would swear loyalty to the Confederacy. Most promotions were slow in coming except during a time of war. It seems they needed men of rank and experience to train green troops, and Colonel Bates was one of the chosen ones. The pay was meager, but it would be helpful in maintaining the Manor House while he was away. He dreaded the hour he had to tell Victoria, but he would wait until after the ball before bearing the sad tidings.

~ ~ ~ ~ ~

On the day the party activities were to begin, the ladies prided themselves on all their accomplishments. Everything was in order and the men folks had even touched up the facade of the Manor House with paint. Paddy had cleaned the gas lamps and trimmed the yard and flower beds to perfection.

Victoria finally opted for the brocaded beige dress and York dressed in pink with tatted lace decorating the bodice. Fashionable ladies, soldiers, lawyer-statesmen, and plantation owners decorated the lawn. The weather cooperated, and after a period of greetings and refreshment, the festivities began. The women played croquet and sipped tea under the oak and magnolia trees, while the men folks amassed for the fox hunt. Colonel Bates was a busy bee, flying from one guest to another, caring for their creature comforts while York joined in on the entertainment and games. Victoria was somewhat sedentary, preferring to chat with the older ladies and swap small talk rather than play games. She did not want to muss the ringlets in her hair. York noticed that Victoria had put on weight since her marriage; however, she was still pretty enough to turn the young men's heads and the older gentlemen's hearts. The Colonel bore her on his arm with pride, cognizant of the fact that he was the envy of old and young alike.

Edwin Sheppard arrived and made a path to York and engaged her in conversation. York hardly recognized him — he was clean-shaven and neatly dressed in his Confederate dress uniform of navy and gray. York had no idea what rank the various medals, stripes and insignias represented. He was taller than she expected, and he walked with a slight limp. At times he leaned heavily on his cane.

"Mr. Sheppard, it is good to see you again, Sir. Have you met the Colonel and Mrs. Bates?"

"Yes, and they were most cordial."

"Aunt Hattie pointed me in your direction and said I would probably find a cool chair on the veranda next to you. I hope you don't mind my speaking in such a manner, but I feel a little out of my element in such an imposing array of gentry."

"If it will make you feel better, I too, am trying to steer away from the crowd." (York was always comparing the young men from the Citadel to Mr. Hampton; somehow, they just didn't seem to measure up to her expectations.) Just listen to all that noise — I would not want to spoil their fun, but I do hope the little fox they are after 'out-foxes' them all."

"Yes," Edwin agreed. "I would say the odds are somewhat uneven." He paused, seeming to be at a loss for words. "Aunt Hattie tells me you like poetry and literature. Have you read the First Essays of Ralph Waldo Emerson?" Edwin continued.

"No, but I would like to read them."

"Then I will send you my copy. It's good reading, and I believe you would enjoy it."

"That's kind of you, Mr. Sheppard."

"I don't get to read much. The war has been a consternation and disruption for me. Oh do forgive me, Miss York, I told myself I would not dwell on the war today."

"I understand perfectly. It's hard to forget when it disrupts every aspect of one's life."

"I suppose there is one aspect of war that is worth mentioning — the *esprit de corps* among our troops. I feel every loss, every pain, and I shouldn't be here. I need to be there fighting alongside them. However, today is a time to laugh, not a time to grieve."

"Then I suppose we will have to make the most of it." York sensed his restlessness as he shuffled his leg often. She realized that he was in more pain than he cared to admit.

"Could I bring you some cool lemonade or tea, Mr. Sheppard?"

"No thank you, Miss York. Your conversation is refreshing enough."

"I'm flattered, Mr. Sheppard."

"Please call me Edwin."

"If you wish."

"Aunt Hattie also tells me you are quite an equestrienne."

York wondered what else Mrs. Comstalk had told him. "I do enjoy riding, but Colonel Bates doesn't like for me to ride alone, and I hardly have time for it now with all there is to do on the plantation."

"If I were here you would not want for an escort. I would seek the pleasure of your company often. I find you most charming, Miss York. The half was not told me by Aunt Hattie."

"I fear Mrs. Comstalk makes bold her assertions."

"She is extremely fond of you. Although I must admit, she is a tough taskmaster. I should know, she was my tutor in my younger days. She thought she was grooming me for a headmaster's job at a local academy in Savannah. I did hold that position for a while, but after joining the Confederacy, I realized I wanted more out of life than that could offer."

"And what would that be?"

"I don't know for certain, I suppose I'm floundering. I have a lot of thinking to do; and what would you like, Miss York?"

"I would love to go to Italy or Paris to pursue the fine arts or write books."

"A noteworthy goal, I would say."

"It's not likely that I will get to travel with the war going on."

"The war will not last forever, Miss York."

"Yes. I realize that this too, shall pass."

"Yes, indeed. When I lost my wife, Emma, I thought life was over for me. I later realized that life was duty, not beauty."

"Oh but I want it all, life and beauty, as well as duty."

"And I pray you will have it, Miss York."

"There are so many beautiful things in the world. Why must life always be ugly and wearisome? I choose to smell the flowers, gaze at a beautiful sunset, listen to the whippoorwill's call, or watch the eagles soar. That's what I want to do, Edwin, soar through life, not crawl!"

Talk came easy with Edwin, and he was less apt to be censorious than most folks. York enjoyed his company, but Victoria and Mrs. Comstalk read more into their meeting than was warranted. She had no romantic inclination toward him whatsoever. She couldn't help comparing him to Tray Hampton; he certainly did not have Tray Hampton's sense of humor and resolve, but he was pleasant enough. He promised a return visit before reporting for active duty again.

The party had gone well and everyone seemed to enjoy themselves. They would all be leaving on the morrow, and the Colonel and Victoria would get some much-needed rest. York sensed the Colonel had something on his mind, for he was in deep thought when she approached him at intervals. Victoria was too preoccupied with the guests to notice.

York had avoided Mr. and Mrs. Foy, and the subject of Andrew, as much as possible. She didn't know if they had heard from him or not, and she dared not ask, nor did she want to ask. His behavior had been most alarming, and as far as she was concerned, he was *persona non grata* around the plantation.

Chapter 20

In the midst of the crisis between Victoria and the Colonel regarding his decision to join the Confederacy, York made herself scarce and saddled Duchess for a morning ride. She knew the pattern...Victoria would cry and pout for awhile, and then finally resign herself to the inevitable. Colonel Bates would more than likely be training young recruits at the Citadel and be far removed from the battlefields. This should be a great comfort to Victoria; nevertheless, she would miss him just the same. The Lord had taken care of them thus far, and York had no doubt He would see them through the worst times. Aaron and Paddy would bear the work load around the plantation. It wouldn't be easy, but with the Colonel's income and Mrs. Comstalk's boarding fee, they could manage the taxes; their daily sustenance would have to come from somewhere else. Sudie Mae would need money for a doctor when she delivered and there would be other expenses all along. York thought she would try to get a job tutoring children on the neighboring plantations. After all, it was no disgrace to be poor.

When she proposed this to Victoria, Victoria told her tutoring would be beneath her station. "Victoria, I perceive you are much too proud," York scolded. "It's time someone in this family came to the realization that there is a war going on and it may not be over for a long time. We can't sit here and do nothing. Now I have given it much thought: either I go to work, or we make room for more boarders. People come and go here at the Manor House. We should start charging an overnight boarding fee."

"Have you lost your senses, York? These folks are our guests!"

"Guests or not, we can't continue to feed them all."

"Where is your sense of hospitality?"

"And where is your sense of priority?"

"I won't have it, York; I simply will not have it."

"We shall see Victoria, we shall see."

It was no use trying to talk to Victoria about scaling down. She only saw what she wanted to see; however, York convinced the Colonel that for her to go to work was the only expedient thing to do. It would give her time away from the plantation during the day and the hours were such that would allow her to travel the short distance to and from her work. York was excited about the prospect of earning her keep. She worked on her wardrobe for the next few days, being careful that her clothes did not look too young or too matronly. She badly needed shoes, but her boots would be fine until another shipment came through the warehouse in Charleston.

Meanwhile, Mrs. Comstalk was instrumental in procuring an interview for her with a family of twelve children. It would only be temporary employment, for the Jacque Marcellus family were of French descent and would be returning to France sometime in the not-too-distant future. She would be teaching the children how to speak English. Mr. Marcellus had leased the old Wythe plantation that had fallen into disrepair in the neighboring low country. York remembered the old mansion sequestered in the dense forest around the bend of the river; it was approximately two miles distant from the Foy plantation.

York had to admit she was less than confident about her first interview, but she steeled herself for rejection in case all did not go well. She fussed with her hair that morning and walked back and forth in front of the mirror several times before pronouncing herself presentable. She would drive her Father's one-horse carriage today, but considering the muddy roads during the rainy season, she would have to ride Duchess to and from work.

Victoria watched her leave. She had no control over York, but she knew that if Father and Mother were living, they would be proud of their little girl right now. The Colonel had been wrong in shielding Victoria with regard to their financial status, for she had not grasped the gravity of the situation. At least the Colonel had saved the plantation from total ruin and Victoria was grateful. Many plantation owners had lost their plantations and left the low country. If she had listened to the wisdom of Father and not been so stubborn, the family would more than likely have fared better elsewhere. Victoria sighed...if only she had half the sense that Father and York possessed, she would have realized sooner what her life had been...vanity. All is vanity!

York returned with her chin held high and her confidence elevated. "Did you get the job, York?" Victoria asked.

"Indeed I did. I start on Monday."

~ ~ ~ ~ ~

The Marcellus children were delightful little stairsteps and very well behaved. The older ones (André and Johanna) appeared to be eager to learn. York found that she was enjoying herself immensely. Mr. and Mrs. Marcellus spoke very little English and often called on her to interpret for them at the market place. They were jolly souls, a little eccentric, but nice. One's culture dictates one's behavior, she supposed. The pay was not quite what she had expected, but she was thankful to have the position.

York had to pass the Foy plantation going to and from work; and it was inevitable that she would meet up with the Foys one day on the road. Mr. Foy pulled his buggy to the side to let her pass, then motioned for her to stop. She was tired and not interested in getting into a long conversation, but she couldn't keep avoiding them forever.

"Thought you might want to know," Mr. Foy said sadly, "me and the Missus are on our way to the hospital. My boy has come down with bilious fever."

"Bilious fever? Andrew?"

"I'm afraid so. Sounds pretty serious. Thought you might want to know."

"Is there anything we can do?"

"No. Thank you just the same. Well, I'll hurry along now." He tipped his hat and was gone.

~ ~ ~ ~ ~

"Did you say Andrew Foy has bilious fever?" Victoria asked.

"Yes."

"Well I'm not surprised from what I hear about the unsanitary conditions in our army camps. The Colonel says they are extremely lacking."

"You would think the Sanitary Commission could control the situation."

"They try, I suppose, but diseases run rampant."

"Do you think Andrew will recover?"

"More than likely, unless they have waited too long to see a doctor. They will probably isolate him for several days to be sure of his condition."

"I do wish him well. I have mixed emotions regarding Andrew. I dislike him and feel sorry for him at the same time."

"That's natural. After all, you were friends for a long while."

"Yes, but I will never feel the same way about him again."

"Oh by the way, I almost forgot, a package came for you today. It's probably the book you expected Edwin to send. Mandy put it upstairs in your room."

"Thank you. I can hardly wait to read it."

"I also got a letter from Colonel Bates. He is certainly basking in his element. He enjoys the work, but says he is missing us all very much, and assures me that he will not be gone any longer than necessary."

"That is good. Give him my warmest regards, Victoria. I will come down to dinner shortly after I have freshened up."

To York's amazement, the package was not from Edwin, but from Tray Hampton! Her hand trembled from excitement as she tore open the wrappings. It contained a lovely volume of poetry and a letter. He had placed a rose inside the letter and labeled it, "A rose for York." His message read:

Dear Miss York,

Time was of the essence and did not permit me to bid you a proper goodbye. I sought to explain to you, but with a bounty on my head, I could not take the chance of being discovered, for it might have brought undue harm to all of you and sorely grieved my spirit.

Spring is lovely here in the English countryside. I plucked a rose from the Lyons' palatial gardens for it reminded me of you as I last saw you — dressed in white, as a bride adorned for her husband, and with the most becoming natural blush on your lips and cheeks. I knew this phantom rose would fade by the time you received it, therefore, I am describing it to you. It is of the purest white, with a tinge of pink on its petals. Its perfume would revive the goddess, Psyche, from her state of unconsciousness. I am sending it to remind you that no suitor has the rite of passage to your affections while I am away.

I can see you bristling already at my presumptuousness. I must say, anger becomes you. Upon my honor, I will not apologize, for I fully expect to return and I intend to marry you one day!

Sincerely,
Tray Hampton

"What tenacity! What sophistry!" York scoffed. She didn't know if it was his presumptuousness, or the fact that he had plucked a rose from Dorthea Lyons's garden that angered her the most. He had never mentioned Dorthea Lyons to her, but he had spoken of her once in Victoria's presence; and now he was plucking roses from her garden! "Mr. Hampton, Sir," she mumbled underneath her breath, "we shall see who is the better fighter in the 'war of roses.'"

Dear Mr. Hampton,
Your letter was most enlightening. The rose is beautiful in death, for it lies silent and still, as a testimony of renewal and friendship. Had it arrived earlier in full bloom, I might have worn it on my breast the night of the Ball hosted by Colonel and Mrs. Bates. We had such a lovely time, and Mrs. Comstalk's nephew, Edwin, came over from Savannah. The ladies were simply infatuated with him and I must admit he was a marvelous dancer, but not half as suave as you.

As far as your intentions are concerned, I regret that my feelings for you are not mutual; however, I might be persuaded to write you again if you promise not to pluck another rose from Dorthea's garden.

Mr. Hampton, Sir, you really are incorrigible!

Sincerely,
York Selassie

Tray thought he detected both anger and jealousy in York's letter. It had not occurred to him that she might believe he was seeing Dorthea again. He was only a member of the bridal party
attending her wedding. If this was what it took to make York jealous, then he pacified himself with the thought that he was at least
making some progress with her. Had she not agreed to write him?
And, who was this 'Edwin person'?

What nerve...she called him Edwin. First Andrew, and now
Edwin...he didn't think he would approve of the old chap. He
vowed he would continue to woo York with pen and ink.

Dear York,

How long have I had the pleasure of your acquaintance — a
year or more? My Lady, it is time you showed me the proper
respect and called me by my first name, or is that only held in
reserve for your Southern gentlemen friends?

(He was jealous! York had accomplished what she had set out
to do. It pleased her to no end. She read on. His letter took on a
more somber tone.)

How it grieves me that you are so far away. From what I read
in the papers, the South is really taking a beating from the North.
Do proceed with caution at all times, my dear girl. Would that I
could rescue you from the terrible ravages of this war.

Now as to my present state, I will soon be finished with law
school and will sail to Washington as a material witness, along
with many others, in the international piracy scandal. It will
prove to be a valuable experience, but seeing the Rector again will
be most unpleasant, I surmise. Enough about me. Do write often.

Love,
Tray Hampton

P. S. I thought roses were a favorite of yours. Would you

prefer heather instead? Dorthea Lyons is happily married and has recently moved to Ireland.

~ ~ ~ ~ ~

Dear Mr. Hampton,

Your postscript was a trifle surly, but I must concede you have won this round in the 'war of roses.'

Please be advised that I will be praying for you during your time of duress during the piracy trials. I am certain justice will prevail.

Yes, the war is drawing closer to our doorstep. Sometimes it seems so far away, and yet, the shortage of material goods and food belies the fact. The cannons can still be heard for miles around, but so far, our Navy has been able to keep the Federals out of Ft. Sumter. I do not mean to imply that we are in immediate danger. We are quite safe here in the low country and doing well.

Sudie Mae gave birth last night to a fine baby boy. They named him Nathan, meaning, gift or given. We delivered him ourselves, for the doctor was late arriving due to a horrendous rain storm that mired his buggy in the mud — all the way to the axle. Later, when the doctor finally arrived, he pronounced both mother and child fine.

I have taken a tutoring position over at the old Wythe Plantation. A family from Paris by the name of Marcellus, has leased the property until after the school year ends. They will be returning to France next summer. They would like for me to visit them upon their return. It would afford me great pleasure to do so, but in our present straits, the possibility eludes me. I was remiss in not thanking you for the book of poetry. Be assured, it will find a prominent place in my library.

Sincerely,
York Selassie

P. S. I lied to you about Edwin. I did not "trip the light fantastic" with him, for a war injury has left his limb temporarily stiff.

Chapter 21

York received another book from Tray Hampton. This one was beautifully illustrated with watercolor sketches of English gardens, scenes along the Thames River, and castles with grandiose archways. One sketch was of a secluded village cafe overlooking a large body of water. Tray had written a message on the opposite page that fairly took her breath away...

My Sweet York,

Picture just the two of us seated at a table in this secluded setting overlooking this body of water. There is a fountain close by and its song softly serenades us as we dine in quiet ambience. Envision the flowers growing nearby, and magnolias blooming overhead with dark, thick leaves. There is no need for reciting poetry, for poetry is all around us. Listen to the song of the lark, feel the gentle breeze, and watch the geese fly toward the setting sun to find a resting place.

Would that I could take wing and fly to you, for there my heart would find a resting place, if only you loved me, too. Believe me when I say I have loved you deeply from the very first time I saw you. Will you marry me? My intentions are honorable.

With Unfeigned Love,
Tray Hampton

York was ecstatic! She treasured the letters she received from Tray. She would not share their contents with anyone — not even Victoria. His letters were "a garden enclosed," meant for her eyes only. Dare she take Tray seriously? She was cautiously optimistic. She wasn't sure how to answer him...

Dear Mr. Hampton,

Your letter left me breathless. I don't quite know how to answer your declaration of intent. I must say I have much to think about.

To say your note was picturesque is an understatement — it transported me back to happier times before the war, when we could sing a peaceful song about the South in all its brilliance. When I am weary at the end of a long day, I read the books and letters you send and they comfort me.

Keep telling me you love me and perhaps one day I shall believe you.

Sincerely,
York Selassie

~ ~ ~ ~ ~

Dear York,

You are the most stubborn woman I have ever known. Shall I grovel at your feet in order for you to believe that I love you? Then I shall. Now, how is that for abject humility?

Oh my darling, you have made me so very happy to know that you will consider my proposal. I will await your decision. Think of me and take all the time you need, but I beg of you, speed a word of love to me. I miss you terribly.

With Heartfelt Love,
Tray Hampton

~ ~ ~ ~ ~

Dear Mr. Hampton,

My modesty would not possibly allow me to speed a word of love to you without commitment, lest you think me an unchaste woman. I am not quite ready to give you my answer. But I will foreswear that I hold you in the highest regard and I, too, miss you. Patience has its own reward.

Sincerely,
York Selassie

My Darling York,

How could I possibly think of you as an unchaste woman? You are the most pure and chaste creature I have ever known. I could not wish for anything more. I have no doubt you would expect me to be of unsullied reputation as well. I believe, my dear girl, we are even on all scores.

I will be patient with you, my beloved, and I will await your answer.

With Sincere Love,
Tray Hampton

Tray's letters became York's lifeline. They were a welcome respite from her mundane existence on the plantation. Life was becoming more difficult, and food shortages continued to plague folks in the low country; and if these hardships weren't enough, inflation was still on the rise — flour was almost a hundred dollars a barrel.

Occasionally, when Victoria and York did not know where their next meal was coming from, a package would appear at the door of the Manor House. There would be no return address. Sometimes the package contained items that were impossible to get at the market, or goods that had been smuggled over the enemy lines. No one knew who had sent them. Colonel Bates rarely sent packages home, for he found they were often tampered with and sometimes never reached the plantation at all; so the source of these goods was becoming quite a mystery.

Soldiers scouting for food and horses for their Calvary, canvassed the neighborhoods. To refuse them was labeled unpatriotic; as a result, food supplies at the Manor House began to dwindle as well. Most of the chickens on the plantation had disappeared, and Paddy and Aaron would hide the horses in the fields away from the barn, or in a dense grove of trees during the daytime, but it was inevitable that some of them would be discovered sooner or later.

A Confederate officer and his scouts came through one day at dusk. They badly needed horses. And Victoria and York had no other recourse than to give them permission to take them. They instructed Aaron to saddle them up — horses weren't good without saddles. The quartermaster leading the party was extremely polite and apologized for the inconvenience. He asked Aaron about the dappled mare.

"What about the mare, young man?"

"Don't think you want to take her, Sir. She is stubborn, that one. Throws every rider who tries to mount her, except Miss York. That mare has a bad hip, too. Ain't fit for nothing."

"Well, bring her out and let me have a look at her."

Aaron tried to stall as long as he could. He knew that York prized Duchess above all the others and he didn't know if his plan would work or not, but he had to try. He opened his pocket knife and cut a plug out of the calf of his leg, mixing his own blood with manure in the stall, and spreading it on Duchess's flank. Perilous times called for drastic measures. At least that was less painful than a hanging if he refused to let the officer have her. He and Paddy would need that horse come plowing time if things got any worse around the plantation. Aaron had a way of making Duchess falter her steps, and when the quartermaster saw her, he wheeled his horse around and remarked to the others that he reckoned she was good for nothing but soap.

York and Victoria stood in the doorway of the Manor House and watched them ride by. The officer tipped his hat at them and told them he was much obliged.

Victoria began to whimper. "Oh York, that was all we had left of Father."

"I know, but men's lives are at stake. How could we refuse them? At least they weren't scalawags."

Aaron came walking up to the big house and they noticed the red stain soaking his pant leg.

"Aaron, what have they done to you?" York cried.

Aaron explained what had happened, and prided himself on the fact that his scheme had worked. York all but embraced Aaron while telling him how proud she was of him for saving Duchess. Victoria told him to come into the big house and let Mandy take care of his wound. York was continually amazed at the loyalty of the Lewis Family. She wondered what the Confederates would come after next! She hoped they wouldn't try to recruit Aaron.

Colonel Bates arrived home on leave too late to save the geldings, but having him around for awhile lent an air of security. He wasn't too happy about the horses. Nevertheless, he knew the girls had done the right thing. The war was hard on everyone, and you can't fight a war without food and horses, he reasoned. He would be on leave for a month, and then return to the Citadel in Charleston to train a new round of recruits. The Manor House was approximately ten miles from the city, and he didn't find it feasible to ride twenty miles a day back and forth to the plantation. In wet weather, the roads were rutted and muddy; and, he had to admit, his old bones weren't what they used to be. Therefore, he had taken a room in Charleston near the Citadel. Victoria grieved that he was so near, and yet so far away. Colonel Bates allowed it was getting harder and harder to leave the girls alone. If they didn't need the currency so badly, and there wasn't such a shortage of men, he would resign his commission. At any rate, he felt the girls were much safer on the plantation than in the city proper.

~ ~ ~ ~ ~

Edwin Sheppard made good his promise to visit the plantation again. He was looking well and was somewhat more relaxed. He drove York and Victoria into Charleston for a day out with Colonel Bates. For lunch, they chose a prominent seafood restaurant near the waterfront. York thought of Mr. Hampton and wished he were seated by her in this secluded corner, instead of Edwin. Edwin was considerate enough, but he had more of a restless nature than Tray. It seemed to York that he was punishing himself for enjoying a day of relaxation, but he and Colonel Bates appeared to be getting along well.

Victoria hoped York would warm to Edwin and their relationship would grow into something more than friendship. York was deep in thought as she looked out over the bay area. It was Edwin who broke her reverie. "The fair lady is pensive today."

"I'm sorry, Edwin, did you say something?"

"I brought you the book I promised." It was carefully wrapped and tied with a blue ribbon.

"Why, thank you, Edwin, you're very thoughtful."

"I know I promised to send it, but giving it to you in person is even better. I would love to see you again, Miss York, if fate allows it."

"That sounds ominous, Edwin."

"Not really. I just don't know where I will be sent next. I fully intend to return to my unit in a few more days. After the war is over, I would like to think that our relationship could blossom into something more."

York didn't know any delicate way to tell Edwin that their relationship had no future. Why were most men so anxious to rush blindly into a relationship?

After they returned from their outing in Charleston, York asked Victoria if she might have a word with Edwin alone. "Edwin, I shouldn't have gone with you today, but I must say it has been a lovely outing. One does not get to leave the plantation often. I am fond of you, and it was not my intention to deceive you, but I am betrothed to another." There, she had said it!

"Betrothed?"

"Yes, that is, Mr. Tray Hampton has asked for my hand in marriage. He is in England as we speak. I haven't given him my answer yet, nor have I told Victoria or Colonel Bates, so you see this is somewhat a delicate matter."

"I see." York noted the disappointment in his face. "Well, Miss York, all I can say is that Mr. Hampton is a man to be envied."

"That compliment is more than I deserve, but I thank you for being so understanding, Edwin."

Chapter 22

D^{ear York,}

The days come and go and I do not hear from you. Are you all right, my beloved? I live for the joy of your letters that cheer me so. Do tell me all is right with us. I fear that life will lose its savor if I don't hear from you soon, and know that you love me and have accepted my proposal of marriage. But of course, I promised you I would be patient, my love, and I will, but please speed a word of encouragement to me. I took the liberty to write Colonel Bates and voice my intentions to marry you.

I long to look upon your beautiful face and see myself mirrored in your lovely eyes, so close, just we two, and kiss your soft, fragrant lips. It is not of lust that I seek this token, but as a seal and promise of my love for you, perchance you feel as I do.

All my love,
Tray Hampton

~ ~ ~ ~ ~

Dear Mr. Hampton,
Considering you have written Colonel Bates and voiced your intentions toward me, I suppose I must tender a word of encouragement to you. I do not deny that I feel a romantic attachment to

you; however, I cannot at this time tell you if I will always feel as I do now, or if my feelings are more than just a dream, or "love-in-a-mist." Surely, you must think me a feather in the wind!

But I will tell you this, Mr. Hampton, that the prospect of the aforementioned seal of promise sounds shamefully enticing.

> *Sincerely,*
> *York Selassie*

~ ~ ~ ~ ~

Dearly Beloved,

Why must you toy with my emotions when I am so far away from you? Nevertheless, I must admit, I enjoy the chase.

You say you are a feather in the wind? Oh no, my love, you are so much more. You are a crown of glory that tests the patience of my manhood. When I am near you, you bring out the best and the worst of me. I cannot explain love, for it is a mystery of time immortal, but I have prayed for the day that you would warm to my affections, and am I to believe that the day has arrived?

Whether your affections for me are a dream, or "love-in-a-mist," my darling York, when you awake, I will still be there and awaiting your pledge of love and matrimony.

> *With Unfeigned Love,*
> *Tray Hampton*

~ ~ ~ ~ ~

More than once in the summer and fall of 1862, the Confederates sent the Union forces retreating toward Washington, but in September the tides turned. With the Battle of Antietam came the bloodiest day in the military history of the United States, as the Confederates were stopped by the North's superior Union forces. The newspaper reported that 26,000 men were dead, wounded, or missing. General Lee withdrew his forces further inland.

It was about this time word came to the Selassie household that Andrew Foy had passed away. After his bout with bilious fever, he caught pneumonia and died. York was saddened; and she thought about Mrs. Foy, remembering what she had said to Andrew as he went off to war — "Don't come home unless you win the war." It was a terrible thing to say to your loved one, and at the time York thought less of her for saying it, but she surmised that it was all said in the heat of patriotism. At any rate, she would console them as best she could.

The Foy's friends came in droves and as the slaves sang over the funeral bier, their haunting strains wafted over their tired and grieved faces. Harmonious melodies and groans were interspersed, lending an air of surrealism to the low country. Apparently, Andrew was well thought of among the slaves.

~ ~ ~ ~ ~

Not long after Andrew's death, it became apparent Mrs. Foy was slowly losing her mind. Mr. Foy was beside himself; he had not only lost Andrew, but he was losing the comfort and companionship of his wife as well. There were almost as many soldiers dying from sickness as were being killed on the battlefield. Many things York didn't understand, but she learned to accept them as God's permissive will, and she dared not question the Almighty. Each day was a trust from God; she vowed to walk in the light thereof, despite her circumstances.

York saddled Duchess and sought seclusion underneath the "old man with a beard." September was her favorite time of the year. She watched the leaves fall and ride the breeze in an autumn frenzy. Some hung tenaciously to the tree limbs, reluctant to turn loose; others eagerly awaited their doom. She watched them float by on the Ashley River like little colorful rafts, exploring the recesses of the inlets and eventually trapping themselves in the tentacles of tree roots along the bank.

Oh, how she wished for another autumn day with Tray Hampton! Her thoughts were legion. She realized she truly was falling in love, else how could she explain that everywhere she went, she was reminded of him. Until now, she had no one with whom to compare him. He was gentle, yet assertive; of unblemished character; intelligent; and challenging. Was not this all she had hoped for in a mate? But how could she be sure he was the right one, and how could they ever really get to know one another other than by letters? Was this a case where faith and trust must be exercised? All this and more she tried to sort out.

~ ~ ~ ~ ~

Dear Mr. Hampton,

After much prayer and thought, I am writing to tell you I am awake now. But was it a dream that I dreamed, or did the most eligible bachelor in all of England ask for my hand in marriage? If this be true, I wish him to know that this is the hardest decision I have ever made in my life; and I would like for him to know that my final decision will be based on faith and trust, and not just the tongue of my foolish heart. I trust that his feelings are reciprocal.

Love,
York Selassie

~ ~ ~ ~ ~

Dear York,

Oh my love, I am appalled that you would think that my feelings could be anything else but reciprocal. To say that I am happy could never describe my feelings at this time. I am overwhelmed with both love and desire for you!

I will come to you, some way, somehow. I will find a time for us. But in the meantime, I will carry your promissory note of love and affection as a buckler and shield against all odds that would seek to separate us from the pledge of love I promised you — a pledge that I fully expect to collect when I see you again!

With Unfeigned Love,
Tray Hampton

~ ~ ~ ~ ~

York contemplated a trip abroad in the future, but it was contingent upon the war and her personal finances. She did manage to save a small sum of her salary each month, providing an emergency didn't set her back; however, it was pittance compared to the amount she would really need in order to subsist. In the meantime, she would have to trust that Mr. Hampton would find a way to come to her. At present, she feared for his safety, should he return to the South. It seemed to her that theirs was a fatal attraction.

How ironic, she thought, Tray Hampton was touted as courageous and heroic in the eyes of England and the United States, but a man with a bounty on his head in Charleston — and naught of this his own doing! How long would it take for justice to prevail?

"York," Victoria chided, "why didn't you tell me that you and Mr. Hampton were secretly pledged to one another? Surely, you must know that I am interested in everything that concerns you and your future happiness."

"I'm sorry, Victoria, the time was not right. And, as far as my marriage to Mr. Hampton is concerned, I have not yet given him my final answer."

"You will say 'yes,' of course."

"Please Victoria, must you press me, also?"

"I don't understand you, York. Father thought very highly of Mr. Hampton. I know this would have pleased him."

"Yes, but considering the war and our present circumstances, we may not see one another for a very long time. Would it be fair to ask Mr. Hampton to wait until the war is over to marry me, when even now he is pressing me for a decision?"

"Don't underestimate Mr. Hampton. If he really loves you, I have an idea he would wait as long as it takes."

"Life is a puzzlement. I try to fit all the right pieces together, but nothing seems to work anymore."

Chapter 23

The war front did not look promising; however the news was not always in the Union's favor. The Northern Army of the Potomac in Virginia had suffered a costly defeat at Fredricksburg. The newspaper reported 12,653 Union losses; it didn't state how many Confederate losses there were. York read that General Robert E. Lee was quoted as saying, after the battle of Fredricksburg, "It is well that war is so terrible, or else we would grow too fond of it."

It seemed to her that the whole nation was "staggering like a drunkard." Congress was planning to enact its first draft that would affect male citizens aged twenty to forty-five. For three hundred dollars or more, the rich could provide a substitute. This was causing unrest and rioting up North. The Northerners complained that the blood of a poor man was just as precious as that of the wealthy. York concurred.

President Lincoln was finally expected to sign the Emancipation Proclamation to free the slaves in all territories held by the Confederates. This was the right thing to do as far as York was concerned. She didn't question the veracity that "all men are created equal," but questioned the timing of it. The North was conscripting slaves to fight in the war and promising them substantial rewards. This would bring more hardships to the South.

The old grandfather clock "talked back" to York, reminding her that the Marcellus children would be up early, and primed for their English lessons. She hurriedly laid the paper aside, gulped down her coffee to the dregs, and bade Victoria goodbye. She didn't want to be late under any circumstances.

It was the middle of December, and it seemed that the temperature had dropped twenty-five degrees since the previous day. York pulled her cape tighter around her shoulders and secured the hood. The wind was vying for superiority.

Aaron had roused a sleepy Duchess from her stall and harnessed her to the buggy. "It's a cold day, Miss York. You best wrap up in that horse blanket. It doesn't seem fitting for a lady of your stature to be out on a day like this."

"I will be fine, Aaron."

"Now do be careful, and if you're late, I'll be out looking for you."

"That's comforting, Aaron. Thank you. And you stay clear of those Confederate soldiers. We wouldn't want to lose you."

"Don't you worry, Miss York, I'll take care of business on this end." York was satisfied he would, too. She voiced a silent prayer for the Lewis Family.

York passed the Foy Plantation. All was quiet. The hoarfrost on the tall pines reminded her that Christmas would soon be here. A mile or more down the road, Duchess began to snort and grow restless. She always acted this way when she picked up the scent of a wild animal or some stranger along the way. York strained her eyes at the thick brush and pines. She thought she saw a flash of white darting in and out among the trees. She pacified herself with the thought that it was probably a white-tailed deer foraging in the forest, but when Duchess halted, York's hair stood on end. She heard a low moan, and it wasn't the wind; Duchess was smarter than she was. She heard the strange sound again, saw a flash of white, and watched it disappear. She didn't believe in ghosts like some of the superstitious folks in the low country; nevertheless, someone or some animal was stalking her.

"Who's there?" she called out. No answer. She called even louder. Her voice reverberated throughout the forest floor. No answer.

"Show yourself," she cried. Presently, a blanched face, set in a mass of tangled gray hair peered out at her — "Mrs. Foy? Mrs. Foy! What are you doing way out here in your nightgown and barefooted! You will catch your death of cold. Come. It's me, York."

"York?"

"York Selassie. Don't you know remember me?" York could see she was totally out of her wits.

"Sh-h-h-h, girlie. They are over there!"

"Who, Mrs. Foy, who?" York looked in the direction she was pointing and saw no one.

"It's them all right...them Yankees...got my boy...."

"Come with me, I'll take you home."

"Home? Where...home...I don't know where I am..."

When Mrs. Foy would not climb up into the buggy, York handled the situation the only way she knew how.

"Quickly, Mrs. Foy, they are coming for us! Jump up here beside me! Hurry!"

Mrs. Foy literally vaulted into the buggy beside York. York carefully wrapped her in the horse blanket, and Mrs. Foy cried and moaned all the way home.

When they approached the Foy plantation, it was apparent that Mr. Foy and his slaves had been searching diligently for her. Mr. Foy was relieved and could not thank York enough. He said this was the first time Mrs. Foy had wandered so far away from home. From that day forward, Mrs. Foy required watch-care twenty-four hours a day.

~ ~ ~ ~ ~

York was glad it was Saturday and she could stay at home. Yesterday was taxing on her nerves and she ached all over. She hoped she was not coming down with a cold. She would take this time to pen a letter to Mr. Hampton.

Dear Mr. Hampton,

The weather has turned quite cold here in the low country. I am sitting close to the fire, roasting on one side, while freezing on the other.

I trust you are well. I try to keep abreast of what is happening on the war front and around the world, but very little information can be gleaned from our present state of anarchy, and it is not always accurate, as you well know. When will you be sailing to the United States again?

Christmas will be here soon, and you are so far away. Would that a visit could be in order when you are stateside; however, I know it cannot be. Therefore, I must content myself with your letters and look forward to seeing you when the war is over.

I have considered your proposal of marriage and for the life of me, I cannot think of any reason to say "no." Nevertheless, I want you to know that I am not always easy to get along with, and sometimes my weaknesses betray me, and I weep. As far as our relationship is concerned, I will brook no rivals for your affection, now, or in the future. How is that for total honesty and the surrender of my affections into your hands?

Love,
York Selassie

~ ~ ~ ~ ~

Dearly Beloved,
How noble of you to warn me of all your shortcomings! I adjure you to solemnly swear that you will never fail of your shortcomings lest I be forced to confess mine. My Love, my loyalty to you is without guile. How could I possibly pluck a thorn when a rose is within my reach? You are without measure, the most beautiful and loving person I have waited for all of my life. I, of all men, am most blessed.

I don't propose that I will always make you happy or be what you wish me to be, but my darling, I will try. You have honored me with your acceptance of my proposal of marriage, and now I will love, honor, and respect you all the days of my life.

When I come to you again, I do not want to come stealthily, but with the assurance that I am acquitted by the Confederate authorities of all charges against me in the Parvenu incident, and with a free pass through the Confederate lines. Pray that this will be just as I have said. Oh my darling, York, how I long to see you.

All my love,
Tray Hampton

P.S. Dare I ask for a lock of your beautiful hair?

Chapter 24

Christmas was only a few days away. Folks in the low country wished for a lull on the war front and a prisoner exchange that would allow soldiers on both sides to return home for the holidays. Prisoner exchanges were allowed at the beginning of the war, but York did not know if this practice was still in effect.

She could hardly bear another Christmas without seeing Mr. Hampton. She read his letters over and over and occasionally lapsed into periods of depression. She tried to throw off her doldrums by practicing her music and making Christmas presents for the family.

All the presents would be of a homespun nature. Mrs. Comstalk had taught her how to work with tatting in order to make delicate lace, and she had made Victoria a bertha with a wide round collar that would cover her shoulders. She scarcely had enough yarn to knit scarves for the men on the plantation and shawls for Mandy and Sudie Mae. With scrap materials from previous dresses, she made a little gown for baby Nathan. She would bake something special for Mrs. Comstalk to enjoy with her afternoon tea.

There would be the usual hanging of the greens in the Protestant Episcopal Church and a Christmas litany service consisting of prayer, a series of invocations and supplications by the leader, evoking responses by the congregation. This was the one time of the year when many of the low country plantation owners and their families, (including their slaves) all came together and worshiped. York had not met the new Rector, so she didn't know who would lead the services. (It was the duty of every plantation mistress to see to the salvation of her household.) Gifts would be given to the children after the worship services — sparklers, marbles, jump-ropes, or nuts and fruit. York feared many children would go lacking this year with the scarcity of these items. It was just as well. They all needed to realize the true meaning of Christmas was not in the gifts, but in the Giver of Life, Jesus Christ.

York cut off a lock of her hair and sealed it in a letter to Mr. Hampton. She knew he wouldn't get it until after Christmas, but this was all she had to give.

She put on her prettiest dress, a cream colored one, with raised baroque designs stitched in white, gold, and silver threads. It was a dress that had belonged to her Mother, and Mandy had altered it to fit York's small frame. York wore her Mother's dress proudly. She looked quite fashionable with her long black cape and gloves. She pinned a sprig of holly berries to her muff in keeping with the season.

Victoria had a flair for accessorizing her gowns, and the bertha which York had made for her lent an air of elegance to her wardrobe.

The new Rector, Reverend James Masterson, and his wife, Hannah, were a couple in their early thirties. They were very well-dressed and of aristocratic bearings. Reverend Masterson was quite an orator; and unlike the sonorous Reverend Jonas White, he had a pleasant voice and a seemingly humble nature. Hannah complemented him with her sweet, quiet spirit. Their two boys, Seth and Isaac, ages ten and twelve, were adjusting to their new surroundings and reveling in all the attention from the other children.

After the morning worship services, the Rector and his family were invited over to the Manor House for the noon meal. Mandy and Sudie Mae had been frugal enough to put aside a certain amount of stores for the holiday season. It might not be their usual fare, but it would be adequate.

Wild turkeys weren't easy to catch, but Paddy and Aaron had

set a trap to catch a few, and had penned them up for several days until Christmas. Everyone at the Manor House marveled at how juicy and fat they were. The Colonel joked about the turkeys, and this being their "last supper." York thought it might possibly be his *last* supper, for Aaron had confided in her that these self-same turkeys had gotten into the barn and gobbled up most of the winter supply of corn that had been stored in gunny sacks. At any rate, they always seemed to have plenty of sweet potatoes and boiled hominy since these were staple items. York disliked hominy, but there were times when she was thankful for it.

There might be a shortage of food, but there would be no shortage of music this Christmas. When friends and carolers from the church came by, Victoria and York served hot sassafras tea and sweet bread made of acorn flour and honey in the absence of wheat flour and sugar. It tasted better than York thought possible. Fortunately the weather cooperated, and everyone was able to return to their homes before the rains came later that evening.

Mandy was quite good with cookery. She claimed her grandmother was part Indian and had taught her many things about the old ways. Nothing was wasted on the plantation — not even the peelings of fruit or potato skins. She made very good preserves out of fruit peelings and a tasty soup out of the potato skins. In the Spring, she would pick pokeweeds and boil them until they were purged of their bitterness, and then she would cook them with eggs — they were quite good. Walnuts and pecans from the trees on the plantation were plentiful in season. York felt as if they were truly blessed; there were so many hungry people. What would the new year bring?

~ ~ ~ ~ ~

The New Year brought more hunger, and a temporary lull on the war front. York had grown weary with news of the war. She rarely read the newspaper any more, but to pretend the war wasn't there wouldn't make it go away. She envisioned her youth passing her by. She was beset by restiveness. Just when she was about to lose faith in seeing Mr. Hampton again, an encouraging letter came from him.

Dearly Beloved,

Could it be that our prayers will be answered? I wrote to the Confederate Secretary of War, not knowing how my letter would be received, or if I would hear from him at all. I informed him of my situation with regard to the Parvenu incident and the bounty on my head by the Charleston authorities. He was most cordial. He deprecated the fact that the turn of events in the Parvenu case had not been through all the proper courts and was sympathetic to my cause.

He agreed that he would look into the matter further; however, upon mention of Judge Selassie's name, he inquired as to my relationship to the said party, and he advised me that he had known him well. He had the highest regard for your Father. It seems that it is true: one's good deeds follow one, even after death.

He allowed that the letters of marque and reprisal that were issued by President Jefferson Davis in the beginning of the war were not intended to jeopardize the South's friendship with England. He did not want to risk another war with England, but mine was a most unusual case. He did say that he might possibly, upon the approval of the President, provide me with a temporary provisional letter to carry at all times. It would grant me passage through the Confederate lines in order to visit Charleston if I would agree not to bear arms, spy, or aid the enemy in any form or fashion. So you see, my love, my intercourse with the Confederate authorities may prove to be quite fruitful.

I am overwhelmed with joy at the prospect of seeing you as soon as the letter from the President arrives, and I am able to book passage to the United States.

All my love,
Tray Hampton

Mr. Hampton's letter was the balm York needed at that moment. She could not suppress the happiness and joy she felt.

Not even the news that the Marcellus family would be returning to Paris sooner than was expected could quell her excitement. Of course, she would miss the children, but now she had hope, and could look forward to seeing Mr. Hampton again in the not too distant future.

Mr. and Mrs. Marcellus assured York that it was not the man-
ners or customs of the people they disdained, but the low country
was not to their liking and did not suit their constitutions well.
They begged York to accompany them. They offered her three
hundred dollars a month, and room and board to tutor the children. She would have Saturdays and Sundays off as well as all holidays. They would not preclude her from tutoring other children,
if she chose to do so. They enticed her with all the joys of Paris:
architecture, art, fashions, literature, the gardens... It was indeed
a great temptation.

Wasn't it every girl's dream to go abroad? Aunt Penelope had
talked about taking York and Clarissa to Europe one day, but that
was before the war. She would need dresses, shoes, and money for
traveling. It didn't appear that these goods were going to be available for a very long time. There was no way she could afford passage on the ship, even if she could obtain the rest of the items;
consequently, it would be impossible for her to think about it at
this time.

It was several weeks before the Marcellus family let the propo-
sition rest. If she would not accompany them to Paris, perhaps she
would visit them in the future when they had resettled in the
Marais district? York would not give out false hope, but she pacified them by saying she would write and keep them abreast of the
war, and if her circumstances changed, she might possibly consider a pilgrimage abroad.

Meanwhile, York thought about Mr. Hampton and his forthcoming visit. If it took the clipper ship, *Andrew Jackson*, ninety-
eight days to travel from New York to San Francisco, how long
would it take for Mr. Hampton to reach her by steamship? But of
course, the clipper ships were built for speed, and steamships
would probably take longer. She thought of all the pleasures of
marriage and having her own home, but she had to admit she was
nervous about meeting Mr. Hampton after so long a time.

Chapter 25

The Ides of March came, and still there was no word from Tray Hampton. York imagined all sorts of things that might have happened to him: passenger delays; a storm at sea; or hostilities from the South. She was affright with worry and concern. So much had happened since the beginning of the war, she feared she was growing paranoid. Victoria made an attempt to assure her and calm her spirits.

"Everything will be fine, York. I just know it."

"But I haven't heard from him in over two months."

"If he is en route to the United States, it will take weeks for him to arrive."

"Oh Victoria, do you suppose he was not able to get a pass to go through the Confederate lines?"

"It's possible, I suppose. My goodness, you are as nervous as a mail-order bride."

"I feel like one sometimes."

"Do you doubt Mr. Hampton's intentions?"

"Oh no, not in the least. It's just that the choices we make now will affect us in the future. I had my life neatly planned and filed away in the recesses of my mind; and just when I thought I had everything so carefully arranged, it all changed."

"I know it hasn't been pleasant for you, York, living here on the plantation with the Colonel and myself. With the Colonel away most of time, I fear I have leaned on you too heavily."

"No Victoria, you must not think that. I have needed you and the Colonel as much as you have needed me. I only regret my invasion of your privacy. You both have been wonderful to me, but I would not be truthful if I said I didn't want a home of my own."

"This is your home, too. Should you leave, I would miss you terribly."

"And I you, Victoria, but it would be best for all of us."

"Somehow I had not anticipated the time when you would be leaving us. I do hope after you and Mr. Hampton are married, you will reconsider."

"Dear Victoria, did you think I would stay here forever?"

York thought there was more to life than this. She would find it.

As she thought on these things, a wagon hearse carrying a wooden coffin rolled up to the Manor House. Victoria and York were panic-stricken. Victoria was frightened that something might have happened to the Colonel, and York was thinking about Mr. Hampton. Mrs. Comstalk had heard the wagon approach and was looking down from the upstairs window. She reached for her smelling salts and rushed down the stairs. She was certain it was Mr. Comstalk.

Paddy walked out to meet the driver to inquire of his mission. The driver removed his hat and said he was sorry to be the bearer of bad tidings. Paddy was puzzled; he asked whose body was in the coffin. The driver said he didn't know whose body it was — he was just paid to deliver it.

"Oh Lawd! Oh Lawd!" Mandy cried, "some po' soul done gone and met de' Maker!" Mandy believed that before they were laid in the ground, the spirits of the dead hovered all around to haunt folks. She absented herself immediately.

Everyone was hesitant to open the casket. York, Victoria, and Mrs. Comstalk, still in shock, turned their heads and shrunk back. Paddy and Aaron took a hammer and began to draw out the nails. With the screech of each nail being drawn from the coffin, the girls' hearts quivered.

"Well...well...well...," Paddy exclaimed, "dat's one way to smuggle dem' goods. Missus Bates, Missy York, it looks like da' Lord done made His face to shine on us." They opened their eyes and beheld stores of all kinds: staple items of food, cloth for dresses, shirts, and various sizes of leather shoes and boots for the whole household.

The women couldn't believe their eyes. When they had recovered from their fright, they pondered who might be their benefactor.

"Well, whoever it is," Victoria espoused, "we will be eternally grateful. Why, there are enough stores here to feed and clothe the household for the rest of the winter."

"Yes," York agreed. "It seems the Lord is restoring everything the locusts have eaten." Needless to say, they were both relieved.

Chapter 26

After the morning chores, York put on her riding habit and saddled Duchess. It was good to be outdoors on a cool, sunny day and feel the wind in her hair. She wanted to shed her cumbersome petticoats, but thought better of it. Many times Victoria had scolded her for her immodesty in doing so. She had learned to ride side saddle, but she preferred to straddle the horse when putting her through her paces. As horse and rider became one, they fell into a comfortable rhythm. Would that the world be as peaceful as it is on the plantation today, York thought.

She loved the smell of wood smoke sifting through the countryside, and enjoyed gazing at the tracery of bare tree limbs patterned across the sky. Some of the trees were beginning to swell with buds. York hoped for an early Spring. The Manor House was partially hidden by the curve of the Ashley River Road, but she could hear the sound of hammers as Paddy and Aaron circled the plantation, mending fences. They had broken ground for the garden and planted onions, lettuce, and radishes. Poor Duchess had suffered from being harnessed to the plow. Her sides were leaner, but she would have plenty of green grass to eat before long.

York dismounted and sat down beneath the "old man with a beard." She allowed Duchess to forage and follow her around untethered. Many times over, York relived her first meeting with Tray Hampton. She had been prone to hide the deep longing she felt for him and the pleasure she felt at his touch. What had made the difference in their first meeting and their last meeting? Was it his letters, or the fact that she had just grown up?

Would he think less of her and the family if he knew how they had lost the greater part of their wealth and social status since the war? She knew life on the plantation was so different from his life in England.

While most women shielded themselves from the sun, York reveled in it. She lifted her face, and allowed its golden rays to warm her body, soul, and spirit. Her wanderlust thoughts returned to Tray Hampton.

York did not see the sleek carriage drive up to the Manor House, or see Colonel Bates and the impeccable young Confederate soldier disembark from the carriage. She lingered awhile longer beneath the "old man with a beard."

Duchess distracted her by perking up her ears and sniffing the air.

"Come, Duchess, now don't go looking for trouble. It's time we returned to the Carriage House."

"My lady, could you direct me to the Selassie Plantation?"

York froze at the sound of Tray Hampton's voice. She caught her breath and her heart leaped within her breast! She quickly turned, fixing her eyes upon him. He was wearing a Confederate uniform! How could this be? Oh...but he was handsome! His blue-gray eyes read hers, and there was no doubt that the feelings they had shared in writing had blossomed into full fruition. She returned his smile. She must not give in to her emotions but restrain herself as a proper lady should.

"Welcome to the plantation, Mr. Hampton."

Tray caught the essence of her smile. She was so beautiful! He was thinking he would subdue his passion for her, knowing her eristic behavior at their first meeting; but, alas, he ran and embraced her, lifting her off her feet and spinning her around like a leaf in the wind. They gazed longingly into one another's eyes, and then Tray kissed her tenderly on the lips, not once, not twice, but three times! York did not protest too loudly. A shiver went down her spine and she shrank back as she sought to reclaim her modesty.

"Mr. Hampton, Sir, that was quite a whirlwind. If I am to surrender to your charms, please permit me to voice the terms of surrender."

"Of course, my lady."

"You have collected your pledge threefold. Hence, I desire to return to the Manor House and rid myself of this dusty riding habit in order to welcome you in a proper fashion. You see, I did not expect you to arrive today."

"Oh my love, you are like the first flower of Spring with the perfume of fresh air in your hair."

"And you, Mr. Hampton, are traveling incognito, or else you have joined the Confederacy. I pray it is not the latter. I was frightfully worried when I didn't hear from you."

Tray gulped. He had a lot of explaining to do. He would change the subject.

"Forgive me, for worrying you. I had no way of contacting you. Our ship made eleven refueling stops, and when I arrived in Boston, my Uncle Hugh was quite ill."

"I'm sorry. I trust he is better now?"

"He suffers from gout, and quite frankly, he is worrying himself into an early grave by fretting over circumstances he can't change. But enough about Uncle Hugh. My sweet York, we have so much catching up to do."

"Yes, but you haven't explained the uniform."

"Yes, well...I had to see you, York. This is the only way I could come to you. President Jefferson Davis denied my pass. I had to take an oath of loyalty to the Confederacy."

"Oh Mr. Hampton, you are incorrigible!" A tear coursed down her cheek.

"My sweet York, please don't cry. I can't bear seeing you this way. Everything will be all right, I promise you. We can be married right away, and when the war is over, we will settle down anywhere your heart desires."

"But Mr. Hampton, what if you don't come back from the war?"

"Not come back to the woman I love? Look at me York. How could I hope for happiness and a bed of ease when the South is losing the war?"

"But you are an Englishman. Our war is not with England."

"No, my lady, it is not. But ours is a love worth finding, a love worth waiting for, and a love worth fighting for. I want to be near you, to protect you...don't you see, what concerns you and the

South concerns me. I wouldn't be worth an English halfpenny if I didn't fight for you and our future here in the South."

"Your nobility shames me, Mr. Hampton. I...I really don't know what to say."

"Say that you love me and allow me to catch your tears in my vial of happiness."

"I...I...fell in love with an English gentleman...but I suppose I could fall in love again with a Confederate soldier!"

Victoria, the Colonel, Mrs. Comstalk, and the Lewis family were anxiously awaiting the arrival of Tray and York at the Manor House. This would prove to be a time of celebration, and a happy reunion for all.

Dinner that evening was more formal than usual. York and Victoria took great pains with their toilet, wearing their prettiest dresses, and perfuming their baths with lilac soap and rose water. There would be dancing and singing tonight.

After a hearty meal and entertainment, Colonel and Mrs. Bates retired for the evening, leaving York and Tray alone, except for Mandy, who (upon pretense of mending a number of articles of clothing) sat in the hallway straining her ears.

Tray made a formal proposal to York and presented her with a costly diamond ring. They talked on into the night and watched the flames of the fire burn low, sending a rosy glow around the room. Their hearts, in perfect sync, were warm with contentment. Being together again did not seem awkward, but natural and right. Gone were York's schoolgirl anxieties, and as the caterpillar sheds her chrysalis and a beautiful butterfly emerges, even so, York was emerging into a beautiful and mature woman in love.

When the clock struck midnight and the last logs turned to ashes, Tray knew it was time to say goodnight. He brushed York's lips, kissed the nape of her neck and whispered softly, "Tomorrow, my beloved, I will see you on the morrow."

Early the next morning, foreboding news came by a mounted courier. Hugh Hampton was dying. As the carriage bumped across the rutted road, Tray's heart was torn between his beloved York and his Uncle Hugh. Just when he had held York in his arms and extracted a pledge of marriage from her, he was squired away from her in what seemed like a living death.

York was so tender and understanding. He would have felt better perhaps if she had strongly voiced her disappointment, or shed a tear upon their parting, but she had done none of this. Perhaps she had grown hardened to disappointment by necessity.

He knew York had suffered since the war. He had done what he could to throw out a lifeline to the family. This was no small task. The secret underground railroad system used by antislavery people before the war had once again proved to be effective in smuggling goods to the Manor House. This had been a cooperative effort by his friends and associates who were in sympathy with the South. He had not told York and the family about his involvement for fear of hurting their pride. One day soon when they joined hands in marriage, there would be no secrets between them ever again.

Hugh Hampton died shortly after Tray returned to Boston. There were times when their two natures clashed because of varying philosophies of life, but to Tray's surprise, his uncle had left him quite a sum in his Will. He often wondered what he would do if he ever became a wealthy man, but somehow he didn't feel any different. He only sensed gratitude for the overwhelming trust that his Uncle Hugh had bestowed upon him. He purposed in his heart to use the money wisely and never close his eyes to a brother in need. Perchance things went awry and misfortune attended his years of service in the army, York would be well taken care of, for he had left a draft in her name for safekeeping at the Bank of Boston.

Had he been too rash by signing up with the Confederacy? Being an Englishman, he could have remained neutral, or paid a substitute to go to war in his place, but he knew this was not the honorable thing to do.

Meanwhile, York contemplated her situation. She could marry Mr. Hampton and risk losing him to the war, or wait until after the war was over to marry him. But hadn't they waited long enough? Her heart was saying "yes" to his proposal, but her common sense was saying "no." If only she were prognostic and could know what the future held...she appealed to Mrs. Comstalk.

"I see no reason to rush into marriage for a few hours of bliss, only to be torn apart again," Mrs. Comstalk advised. "But let me be quick to say, my dear, that's a decision only *you* can make."

133

"Then you think we should wait?"

"Let me put it this way. You are both young. I don't know how to put it delicately, but what if something should happen to him and you found yourself in a family way?"

"I suppose I would just want to lay down and die."

"I know you will make the right decision, York. You always have."

"Thank you Mrs. Comstalk, you have given me much to think about."

York knew Mr. Hampton would be distraught over her latest decision to postpone their wedding. She prayed that the war would be over soon. She asked the Lord to keep watch over Mr. Hampton while they were apart from one another. She then thanked Him for hearing her, and vowed to give Him all the glory due His name.

York saw Tray Hampton for only a short while before he left to join his regiment in the Army of Virginia. They met at the railroad station in Charleston, exchanged a few words, and York saw him running from car to car waving at her as long as the train was in view. Truly, York concluded, theirs was a love worth waiting for!

Chapter 27

Tray picked up his rifle and haversack, and began another fifteen mile-a-day march to join General Lee's Army of Virginia. They were making an advance into Maryland not too far from Washington. He could scarcely take it all in, everything had happened so fast. Losing his Uncle Hugh, York's postponement of their wedding, and now this. At times when he was tired or despondent, he would take out his pocket watch and stroke the fob he had made out of the locks of York's hair. It still held its sheen. He remembered the diamond of her first tears, the nectar of her kisses, and the stirring in his loins when he pressed her close to him. There was no turning back. He knew York's love and prayers would sustain him.

His regiment had only been involved in a few skirmishes with the North so far, but he was certain the big fight was imminent. Up until this time, it had not occurred to him that he might not make it through the war, and even now, he refused to entertain the idea. He had placed his life in God's hands and this was the greatest comfort of all.

~ ~ ~ ~ ~

Dear York,

The moon is shining over the Rappahannock River tonight, and all is quiet in our encampment. I miss you so much, my love.

I don't know if we will be moving out tomorrow or retreating toward Richmond or Gettysburg to reinforce our troops there. I can't give you my exact location.

Life in the army is different from anything I have experienced before. I am told what to eat, what to wear, when to get up, and when and where to sleep. That's not all bad, but several of my fellow soldiers resent being told what to do, and occasionally rebel. Some have already deserted, and those who have committed capital offenses are tried by a general court-martial. Considering my background in law, I was asked by my superior officers to act as a judge-advocate to certify that the court is correctly conducted. I am not certain this is legal, but in emergency situations this is allowed.

My fellow soldiers are trying to teach me the rebel yell. I don't know how to explain it, but it sounds like the yip, yip, yip of a wild dog, or children at play. At any rate, it sends shivers down the Yankees' spines, so I'm told.

A stodgy little Dutchman has taken a liking to me. His English is very poor, and I have been tutoring him along our march. He is teased unmercifully, but he can hold his own in battle. We had a bad time of it when the Union troops crossed the river to attack us. We sent them back over the river and won a victory for the South. I am unscathed. I dislike being a warmonger, but my love, sometimes war is necessary to put things right. Pray that it will all be over soon. This is a time of testing for all of us. I was saddened to hear that Stonewall Jackson has died from wounds he received in a battle near Chancellorsville. General Lee lamented that he had lost a friend, and "right arm."

All is well in our camp tonight. Go to sleep, my beloved, and sleep well. I intend to do so.

All my love,
Tray Hampton

Upon hearing from him, York wept. Her tears blurred the ink on his letter.

~ ~ ~ ~ ~

On the home front, York scanned the newspaper for causalities of the war. This became her daily routine again, now that Mr. Hampton had joined the Confederacy.

A,   B,   C,   D,   E,   F,   G, H......Hamlet......Hollis......Huddleston......no. There was no Hampton listed among the wounded or dead. She sighed with relief. But so many were missing. She hoped Mr. Hampton was safe in Maryland. She often wondered if she had made a mistake in not marrying him before he left for the war. She studied the ring he had given her. It would be some comfort if only she knew where to write to him. The last letter she had mailed came back to her. Like most Southern women whose loved ones had gone off to war, she could only pray, watch, and wait.

~ ~ ~ ~ ~

The Battle of Chancellorsville had been a very costly one for the Confederacy. It would take months before all the casualties, wounded, and missing could be counted. The North was beginning to look toward the siege of Vicksburg. If they were successful, the Confederacy would be split in two. The entire Mississippi River was now in Union hands. The South's military supplies were rapidly being choked off, as railroads were ripped up like matchsticks, burned, and twisted like spaghetti. Supply warehouses were blown up by the Confederates in order to keep the Union forces from confiscating them. It was in November of that year President Lincoln delivered his *Gettysburg Address.*

Like dominoes, battles were continually being waged and felled, one by one. Chickamauga was a victory for the South, but Memphis, Chattanooga, and Knoxville fell to the Union.

General Grant was promoted to the Commander of the Union armies. He planned to engage Lee's forces until they were destroyed. General Lee needed new replacements, but there were none. Tray Hampton's regiment was pulled out of Maryland to reinforce Lee's men in Virginia. Spotsylvania and Cold Harbor were Lee's last *clear* victories of the war. He had fought General Grant in an inconclusive three-day battle. Grant was forced to retreat temporarily, but pushed on the second time to attack the

Confederate forces, and the North lost approximately seven thousand men in twenty minutes. The only difference in the North and South was that the North had replacements for their wounded, and the South did not.

It was at Cold Harbor that misfortune overtook Tray. He had exposed himself to enemy fire by trying to drag a wounded officer away from the battlefield to safety. How he managed to save him, he didn't know, for little did he realize at the time that he himself had been shot and was losing blood rapidly. The Dutchman had lost part of his cheek and one ear, but kept on fighting until the enemy was routed. Before he blacked out, the last words Tray heard the Dutchman say were, "You jolly goot fellow, I take care of you."

Chapter 28

Colonel Bates came home with a fever and a cough. Victoria and York had noticed he was losing weight. There had been several cases of malaria reported at the Citadel, and Victoria insisted that the Colonel see a doctor at once. The Colonel was dubious, but Victoria was persistent. After a thorough examination, Dr. Moore called Victoria and York into his office.

"Mrs. Bates, your husband is a very sick man."

"Oh pray, doctor, do not tell me it is malaria."

"No Mrs. Bates, it is not malaria. It's consumption."

"Consumption?" Victoria appeared to be stunned.

"But he has always been so strong and healthy." She touched York's sleeve and sank down on a chair to steady herself.

"How far advanced is it, doctor?" York asked.

"That depends... I need to ask you and Mrs. Bates a few questions. How long has Colonel Bates had this cough?"

"For several months, I would say, wouldn't you, York?" York concurred.

"Have you noticed any malaise, chills, weight loss, or night sweats?" They had.

"Mrs. Bates, pulmonary tuberculosis is very serious. In most cases, there is no cure. However, your husband has a fifty-fifty chance in overcoming this disease, if you will follow my advice. You aren't going to like what I have to say, but it is for your own good and your husband's as well."

"Anything you say, doctor. We are willing to do anything to help him regain his health."

"Very good. We need to send him away to a sanatorium. My advice to you is to take him to Red Sulfur Springs, near Richmond, for a complete cure. The waters and diet there are therapeutic and have a quieting effect on the circulatory and nervous system. The environment would be less stressful and afford him rest. Granted, his age is against him, but I believe rehabilitation is the answer."

"How long would he be in rehabilitation?"

"A year or two perhaps, depending on his progress."

"A year or two!" Victoria exclaimed.

"I know this sounds harsh, but there is no inoculation for the prevention of tuberculosis at this time, and your whole household is in danger of contracting this disease. I want you to talk to your husband, and if he is in agreement, I will fill out the necessary papers for you. Just remember, Mrs. Bates, there is always hope. We doctors don't have all the answers. We just prescribe, but the good Lord heals."

Victoria broke the news gently to Colonel Bates, and after much thought, the Colonel agreed to go in order to combat the "great white plague," providing Victoria could find a suitable hotel or boarding room nearby in order to visit him. There was also the matter of packing their trunks, and choosing the mode of transportation for their travel. They decided to go by train as far as they could, and by coach through the deep hollow of the Red Sulfur Springs, near the mouth of a small tributary of Indian Creek, twelve miles from Lowell. As far as Victoria and York were concerned, it could have been on the other side of the world. It would be an extremely tiring trip for the Colonel. York preferred to remain at the plantation and join them at a later date, but Victoria allowed that she needed her now, more than ever, for moral support. Mrs. Comstalk and the Lewis family promised to keep the plantation in "apple pie order," and Aaron promised York that Duchess would be safe in his keeping. Mrs. Comstalk said she would be happy to forward their mail, and keep them abreast of all the happenings in and around the low country.

The day they left, it was a sad parting. They didn't know if the Colonel would ever be able to come home again; "But," they concluded, "without hope, what does anyone have?"

~ ~ ~ ~ ~

Dear Mr. Hampton,

I pray that this letter will reach you. My last post came back to me, so I will try again. It is lonely here without you. Loneliness is not my friend, but my memories of you, are. They are stored in the repositories of my mind. At times, I feast on these memories, and I think how wonderful it will be when we are together again after the war is over.

I dislike being the bearer of bad news, especially at this time when you are facing great dangers every day, but I felt that you should know the Colonel has come down with consumption. As I write this letter, I am on my way to Red Sulfur Springs, Virginia, with Victoria and Colonel Bates. The doctor says he has a fifty-fifty chance of survival. The waters there are reputed to be very therapeutic in the treatment of pulmonary consumption. I understand there are accommodations for visitors, but Victoria and I will find a more frugal place to live during this time. I do not know what my new address will be or how long we will be there. The doctor believes it will be a year, or more, depending on how well his rehabilitation progresses.

As we approach our destination, the countryside is beautifully romantic and picturesque. The road wends around a high mountain that charms the weary traveler. I believe this will be a wonderful place of rest for the Colonel.

Mr. Hampton, please dodge those Yankees and hurry home. Whether we win or lose this war, I want you to know that I am very proud of you.

Love,
York

~ ~ ~ ~ ~

The sanatorium was nestled in a verdant glen, surrounded by lofty mountains. Victoria and York were pleasantly surprised by the warm greeting of the proprietor. He immediately escorted Colonel Bates to the sunny side of the sanatorium and familiarized him with his room and surroundings. After the Colonel had received nourishment and was made comfortable, he did not think he would have such a bad time of it after all.

Victoria and York were shown the visitor's accommodations by Dr. Steinbeck, the administrator of the sanatorium. The buildings were surrounded by promenades, and enclosed by white embellished railings. They found the visitor's rooms to be nice and spacious. Dr. Steinbeck had worked out a financial plan that would not be too burdensome in their present straits. She and York could both stay in the visitor's quarters for the price of one, and would be nearby to visit the Colonel any time they wished. They thought it would be quite comfortable there, as they made preparations to unpack their trunks. A large sugar-maple lent shade to their room and the scenery was breathtaking.

In the village, there were quaint shops, stables, and carriage-houses which were most charming. They found a small restaurant on the north side that served a delectable cut of veal, and field peas — their first warm meal since they had left Charleston.

Chapter 29

Tray Hampton opened his eyes. A dark figure loomed over him. He found himself in a back-woods log cabin sequestered among tall pines. He blinked his eyes and tried to shake the cobwebs from his mind and focus on his surroundings. The black man saw him stirring and proffered him soup, coaxing him to drink.

"You is in good shape, for de' shape you is in, soldier." Tray's leg pained him. It was swollen and feverish.

"Who are you?" Tray asked.

"My back name be's Brown, but mos' folks calls me Bo. Here, take some of this. You ain't et' for bout' seven days." He lifted Tray with his big arm and raised his head.

Tray took a sip and spewed it out.

"By Jove, I should be grateful, but what's in that soup?"

"This here be's rattlesnake soup. Ain't you never tasted it afore?"

Tray was fully awake now. His stomach wretched as he pushed the bowl away.

"Now suh' don't go givin' me no trouble after we'uns done come dis' far. I's bein' paid by de' army to take kere' of you, and I aims to git' you well and collect my monies."

So much for compassion, Tray was thinking.

Tray looked around the cabin. It was sparsely furnished. A string of red peppers had been hung on the wall above the bed to dry, and a rusty teakettle hanging on an iron rod over the fireplace was belching steam and making a hissing sound. There was a bucket of water with a dipper on a small wooden table across the room. Two ragged cane bottom chairs were pulled out from the wall. Tray realized he was thirsty.

"Could I have a drink of water?"

"Now dat' is what I's got plenty of."

It tasted good and refreshed him somewhat.

"How did I get here?"

"A soldier with half his face and one ear missin' brung you here. He say if he not git' back, the litter-bearers be back to git' you in a few days."

Tray remembered seeing the Dutchman with blood splashed all over his face; he thought he was a dead man for sure. "I guess you and he are my heroes, Bo."

"Not me suh', I's just doin' my duty. De' man cut dat' shot outta' dat' leg, and tole' me to not git' it lookin' bad fo' they comes for you. All I had was some corn liquor and dat's all gone now."

"Where am I?"

"Yo' be's hidden out in de wildurness' bout' four miles on de' utter' side of Cold Harbor. You best eat sumpin' and git' yo' strength back."

"Have you got anything besides rattlesnake soup?"

"I's will have soon as I checks my trotlines. Might be I could catch a squirrel iffin' you would let me use de' gun."

"You'd better be a good shot. I only have two bullets in my trousers."

"Oh I's got plenty o' bullets, I jus' ain't got no gun."

"Do you live here all alone in the wilderness?"

"Man, you sho' do ask a lotta questions. I's got my freedom now and I's gonna' stay out here and hides, fore' them Yankees comes thru' and makes me haul tail ta' de' battlefield. Now you quits talkin' and listin' mo.' I's be back in a while. Gotta' go git' us some meat for supper. Ain't got no flour. Dem sutlers wants over a thousand dolla's a barrel — they's sho' knows how to git' rich quick."

"How do you live out here with no food or money?"

"Oh I git's food iffin' I finds a dead soldier. Why dey carries all kinds o' food in them sacks over de' shoulder. See dat' tin over there on de' shelf — well I's got coffee and chawin' tobacco in it. Be times I git' canned oysters or samin' off o' them Yankees, iffin' I git's to em' first."

"So you steal food off dead men, do you?"

"De' way I sees it, we be's even. Dey stole' my two hogs dat' de' Marster give me when he set me free. I sho' do miss dem' hogs. You be's easy now. I be's back quick as I can."

Bo took the rifle and a hand full of shot and went out foraging. Tray tried to raise himself and stand up, but he fell back down on the corn-shuck mattress. He had lost a lot of blood and was extremely weak. The blanket on which he was lying smelled of bear grease — not that he had ever smelled any, but he thought this might be what it would smell like. Poor old Bo gave all he had; he just didn't have much to give. Tray would remember to reimburse him in time. His leg was beginning to throb and red streaks were moving up it. His bandages were soaked, and he had no clean ones to dress it. He knew if he didn't do something, gangrene would set in.

He hoped Bo was having some success. He was; he came in with two fish in one hand and a squirrel in the other, and a big grin on his face. He patted the rifle, and said, "Ain't she sumpin.' We is gonna' have us one mo' fine supper."

Bo proceeded to skin the squirrel and clean the fish. He layered the squirrel in a frying pan, sprinkled it with salt, and cooked it in a small amount of water until it was tender. The fish were hung over the coals and smoked. The aroma in the cabin was such as to make a man's mouth water and his stomach churn; all in all, it tasted good to a starving man.

"Bo, would you happen to have a pen or paper on hand? I want to write to someone who is very special to me."

"No suh', I's never learnt' how to write."

"That's all right Bo, it will just have to wait."

Tray had a miserable night, and Bo could tell he was in a great deal of pain. Bo was thinking, "if de' litter-bearers don't come fo' him soon, Mistah Hampton might jus' be a goner."

"You wants me to leech you Suh?"

"Leech me?" Tray queried.

"Ain't you a dum' one. A leech be dat' small lil' worm dat' sticks to de' skin an' sucks de' poison out."

"I know what a leech is Bo, but if it's a leeching I need, why don't more doctors practice this procedure?"

"Well, best' I's can figure out, they's not as smart as ole' Bo here, I reckon."

"I reckon not, Bo," he chuckled.

The next morning, after a bitter cup of coffee, Tray removed the fob from his gold watch and tucked it into his soiled shirt. He gave the watch to Bo, and asked him to go to town and trade it in for some medical supplies or bring him a doctor.

Bo had good intentions, but along the way he passed a "distillery," and traded the watch for whisky. He didn't return to the cabin that day.

Tray was in agony! He bumped his leg on a chair and the wound burst open and began to bleed again. In pain and desperation, he reached for the string of red peppers over his bed, slit them open with his pocket knife, and rubbed them into his wounds. They burned something awful, but it was nothing compared to what he had already suffered. This stopped the bleeding and gave him a little relief. He applied this remedy off and on throughout the day.

Bo finally returned, stinking like a swamp muskrat and as drunk as a skunk! In a drunken stupor, he hardly noticed Tray, and curled up in a corner near the fireplace and went to sleep.

Tray was thoroughly disgusted and decided to get some help even if he had to crawl. Thankfully, this was not necessary, for the litter-bearers finally arrived and took him to a make-shift hospital somewhere in the wilderness. The doctor dressed his wound in sterile bandages and gave him a pill. He didn't know what the pill was, nor did he ask. It seems that all the wounded were given the same pill, no matter what their injury was. The doctor said the red peppers probably stanched the bleeding and helped to keep down the infection. That night, Tray slept like a baby!

Chapter 30

York spent most of her waking hours strolling along the promenades and reading. Occasionally, Dr. Steinbeck would happen by and inquire as to her well-being. He was a proper gentleman with a stiff bearing, and a hoary head of hair that attested to
his age and years of experience in the health field.

After several weeks of rehabilitation, the Colonel's blood pressure and heart rate had gone down. Victoria hardly left his side.
His color was returning, and his breathing was better. He was
enjoying the warm thermal baths with the exception of the odif-
erous sulfur that assailed his nostrils; however, the spring water
itself was colorless.

Mrs. Comstalk sent a post saying everything was well around
the plantation. Aaron and Paddy had weeded the rose garden, and
the grounds were beautiful this year. Duchess was being well
taken care of and baby Nathan was toddling around and bringing
them all much joy. She also wrote of the rumor going around the
low country that General Lee was contemplating a surrender to
General Grant. Mrs. Comstalk allowed that she, for one, was
weary of the war, and if a surrender was imminent, it could not
come soon enough as far as she was concerned. She missed everyone and hoped the Colonel was much improved by the time we
received her letter.

Mrs. Comstalk had said nothing about a post from Mr.
Hampton. York had to assume that all was well, and he was on the

move again. If he was still in Maryland, at least she was closer to him here, tucked away in the hills of Red Sulfur Springs, than in the low country of Charleston. Bits and pieces of the war news trickled down to her, but rarely did she or Victoria broach the subject in the Colonel's presence. He was there for bed-rest and therapy, and they would see to it he was sheltered from any and all stress that would disquiet him.

~ ~ ~ ~ ~

With the improvement of the Colonel's health, York thought it best she return home. Victoria had settled in and was spending most of her waking hours with the Colonel. Since York did not have a traveling companion, Victoria tried to dissuade her, but to no avail. Victoria had a way of projecting her own feelings of insecurity on to York's resolve, and it had always caused her consternation. Indubitably, York was older now and not entirely as unsophisticated in the ways of the world as Victoria would have her believe.

It was agreed upon that York would catch the train at Lowell, Red Sulfur's principal railroad, but not its nearest point. Dr. Steinbeck made arrangements for her to take a coach into town, and the timing was such that she would not have to wait long before the train arrived at the station.

Upon her arrival, she noted that most of the travelers were either very rich or very poor. Of course, everywhere she went there were wounded soldiers returning home and replacements moving hither and yon to the battlefields. She was seated next to a young lady who was bouncing a baby girl on her lap. The baby cried a lot, and York found it impossible to read. She proffered her help, and the young mother let York hold her. The baby was fascinated with York's jewelry and picked at the ribbons on her ruffled bodice.

"Thank you Miss..."

"York Selassie."

"I'm Sally Hatfield. I have wrestled with the baby all morning, and I was at my wits' end not knowing what to do with her."

"She is a beautiful child."

"Thank you. Her father was killed in the war, and we are going back to Georgia to live with my parents." She drew out her handkerchief as her eyes filled with tears.

"Oh, I'm terribly sorry, Sally."

Sally composed herself. She asked York if she was married.

"No, but I am betrothed to a wonderful gentleman who is a barrister from England." She thought it best to not bring up his tenure of service at this time.

"Sally, why don't you join me for a spot of tea at our next stop?"

"I would certainly welcome that," she responded.

From sheer exhaustion, the baby fell asleep in York's arms.

Having Sally Hatfield to talk to made the journey more pleasant and viewing the countryside was a special treat. It would be good to be home again. She hoped a letter from Mr. Hampton would be waiting for her. She thought about the Hatfield baby and wondered if Mr. Hampton had his sights set on a large family. They had not talked of children, but there would be time for that later. She wanted more than anything else to be a good wife to Mr. Hampton. She guessed it was her Southern upbringing, but she had not even allowed herself to call him "Tray." A warm flush enveloped her at the thought of his kisses that burned on her lips and left her breathless. She was glad Sally could not read her thoughts. The one thing of which she was ignorant, was how to love a man. Victoria said it would all come naturally, and they would learn together.

As the train neared Charleston, she and Sally exchanged addresses and agreed to write one another. It was nice making new friends, and she was excited about seeing old ones. Sudie Mae and Aaron met her at the station. Duchess was hitched to the carriage, and she was in fine form. York patted her soft nose, and Duchess thrust out her tongue and bathed York's face good and proper; the mare smelled of new mown hay. York was glad she had sent a telegram ahead, stating when she would arrive. They talked incessantly all the way to the Ashley River Road; before York realized it, they were at the Manor House and she was being swept up into Mandy's and Mrs. Comstalk's warm embraces.

Chapter 31

The *Charleston Mercury* reported the forthcoming attack on Atlanta. Sherman's army had begun its march to the sea, and much destruction was following in the wake. On the Eastern front, General Lee was still battling General Grant's forces, and contemplating a surrender. This peaked York's interest, and she was hopeful that, win or lose, the conclusion to the war would soon be forthcoming. What she didn't know was that it would be a matter of months before the capture of Richmond and Petersburg (the South's main supply route).

Victoria had written that she and the Colonel had accompanied Dr. Steinbeck to a Ball in Petersburg, and it was most enjoyable. This was their first outing in a long while. The doctor thought the bacillus that had caused the Colonel's disease had been arrested and he was no longer contagious; nevertheless, they were being cautious.

She said the folks in Petersburg were having a grand time, and all the while, bullets were flying less than two miles away. It didn't seem to bother the town folks and the party went on as if nothing was happening. Victoria went on to say that if she had known how close the Yankees were to them, she would have fainted then and there, but they all made it back to the sanatorium safely. Victoria wrote that the doctor was a marvelous dancer, despite his age, and one would have thought he was a *boulevardier* (man-about-town), with all the attention he received from the ladies.

151

York smiled as she read Victoria's letter. She was pleased with the report on the Colonel, and she felt as if they would be returning to the Manor House sooner than was expected.

Sunday morning came, but there were no church services nearby to attend, for a tragic mishap had occurred. Or was it the Lord's judgment? Someone involved in the International Piracy Ring decided to retrieve a cache of stolen arms and gunpowder that had been secretly stashed away underneath the floor of the Protestant Episcopal Church. The intruder was careless, struck a match, and the whole church blew up in smoke and flames. The body of the intruder was so badly burned he could not be identified.

Most of the congregation was still in shock and disbelief, for had the church been full, they would have all perished. Reverend and Mrs. James Masterson were not on the premises at the time, which was an added blessing. The parsonage nearby was still intact, but every window pane, picture on the wall, and most of the dishes had been broken from the concussion of the blast. The Mastersons agreed to stay and help rebuild the church if that was what the congregation wished. At any rate, this incident alone was enough to render Jonas White, the former Rector, guilty of all charges in the international piracy scandal. Without question, York thought, he would face a firing squad or hanging. Was it Sir Walter Scott who said, "What a tangled web we weave, when first we practice to deceive"?

A post from Mr. Hampton finally arrived, months after he had written it. Little did York realize that Tray's fellow soldier, the Dutchman, had found it in Tray's pocket after he was wounded and blacked out. Unbeknownst to Tray, the Dutchman forgot about it, but upon remembrance, mailed it on Tray's behalf. The corners of the envelope were tattered and torn. Mud stains and water circles attested to the fact that it had been handled roughly. York was puzzled over the handwriting on the envelope. At any rate, it was legible, and she was enthralled as she read Tray's letter.

Dear York,

Your letter finally caught up with me. Sometimes our mail is delayed for days or months. Often it does not reach us at all. It was the opium I needed, but I was saddened to learn of the Colonel's state of health. *Give him my regards. Do not be bereft of hope, my love, for I have heard of many cases far more advanced than the Colonel's, and I believe that diet, rest, and quietude play a major role in recovery from this disease. The course he has charted will undoubtedly facilitate a complete recovery. My greatest fear is your exposure to the disease. Do practice caution at all times. Are you eating well and resting during your sojourn away from the plantation? Perhaps it is good that you have been away from the low country during the malaria season.*

Our regiment was called out of Maryland and back into Virginia to reinforce the troops along the James River. We are on the move, and I seldom know from one day to the next where we will be traveling.

On a happy note, I must tell you that a revival has swept through our camp and is spreading rapidly to the other troops. I myself was genuinely affected. I have come to the realization that the Lord has a greater place of service for me than I could ever have imagined. I will tell you all about it one day.

My Darling, I fear we are fighting for a lost cause, but I am not in despair. I must close for now, for darkness has overtaken me. How I long to hold you in my arms...

~ ~ ~ ~ ~

When news came that Union General Sherman had taken Atlanta, the war-weary North took courage. President Lincoln's popularity soared, and this helped him win re-election. He called for the Confederacy electorate in each state to swear past and future loyalty to the Union and promised they could be restored. This fell on deaf ears. The war would go on, but for all practical purposes, the Confederacy had already fallen.

It was mid-December and the Colonel and Mrs. Bates returned to the Manor House for the holidays. The Colonel had regained the weight he had lost and was convalescing well. He realized it would only be a matter of time before General Sherman would move from Atlanta to South Carolina. Southern troops were gathering in Charleston in readiness for a last stand against the Union, and plans were being made for the evacuation of the city. Colonel Bates doubted they would be in the path of destruction, since they were sequestered in the low country, but he didn't want to take any chances. He advised Victoria and York to secret any valuables they deemed sentimental. With fear and trepidation, the girls obeyed. He proposed a trip to a pine resort in North Georgia until after Sherman's troops passed through, but it was the dead of winter. Victoria and York feared the Colonel would have a relapse, considering the summer houses were airy and devoid of insulation from the cold; therefore, they chose to remain on the plantation.

It was during this time that a post arrived from Mr. Hampton. York learned he was recovering from a wound to his leg. As she looked back at the calendar, she realized this must have happened shortly after he had posted his last letter, or about the time she was penning him a letter while traveling to Sulfur Springs. That would explain the handwriting on the envelope of his previous letter. York was beset with anxiety. Tray played down the whole affair and joked that he could still dance and put his arms around her. York was overjoyed that he was better, but at the same time she was bitter over the atrocities of the war. She ran away to ride the dappled mare, and her tears mingled with the dust on her face. She finally released every emotion she had pent up since her Father's death.

~ ~ ~ ~ ~

January saw more desertions from General Lee's army of Virginia. Transportation problems, blockades, severe food shortages, and a lack of supplies plagued the South. Confederate President Jefferson Davis agreed to send delegates to a peace conference to meet with President Lincoln. Davis insisted on Lincoln's recognition of the South's independence as a prerequisite for peace. Lincoln, having the upper hand, refused.

Richmond, the Confederate capital, fell, as did Petersburg. The Colonel did not return to Sulfur Springs, Virginia, for his treatments.

Tray Hampton was among the last of the wounded to return to the battlefield and fight for the South. It was in Virginia that his regiment was soon surrounded, and Grant called upon Lee to surrender. The two Generals met at Appomattox Courthouse and agreed on terms of surrender.

Tray Hampton and his fellow soldiers were stunned when the announcement came that the war was over. They walked around in a daze, mingling with the Northern troops. Some cried, others cursed and mocked, and Tray knelt to pray. They would all be sent home on parole. The soldiers endeavored to quell their excitement by hastily gathering up their meager belongings. They could keep their horses if they had any, and officers could keep their side arms. Tray thought General Grant was generous; he was not the warmonger most folks in the South believed him to be. He was courteous to General Lee and genuinely happy that the war was over. Confederate Jefferson Davis had left Virginia and had gone into Georgia, where he was captured and later released by President Lincoln.

Tray feared that in the fall of Charleston, York and her family might have fallen into the path of destruction. He had heard all kinds of stories about what had happened to Atlanta, and he knew Charleston would more than likely not escape Sherman's wrath. He intended to leave for Charleston as soon as possible, even if he had to walk all the way; so many of the railways had been destroyed that travel was difficult. He clasped his discharge papers in his hand and voiced a final goodbye to his friends; he shook General Lee's hand. General Lee, remembering he had brevetted Tray for his bravery, replied, "Well done, Mr. Hampton, perhaps we will meet again during the reconstruction of our country." Tray didn't see the grand old general again, but he would never forget his sad eyes, as he saluted the last remnant of his troops in the Army of Virginia.

~ ~ ~ ~ ~

The town of Charleston and many of her landmarks had been destroyed by fire. The Confederacy, itself had destroyed much of the city by blowing up buildings and ships to keep the North from capturing them. Poor and hungry citizens in Charleston broke into the arsenal to steal food, and somehow the place caught fire and blew up, killing a number of them. The fire swept to other buildings and parts of the town, while General Sherman's men marched through and cut a swath through the main part of the town, burning and pillaging houses along the way.

At night, standing on the balcony of the stately Manor House, York could see the red glow of the fire reflected on the far horizon, as Charleston burned. Perhaps rain saved many plantations from destruction, for it had rained heavily in the low country the night before; the rain had flooded the roads, making it impossible for wagons and horses to traverse the mud and swamps along the Ashley River roads. York viewed the rain as God's providential care over them.

Confederate soldiers continued to pass by the Manor House on foot, stopping by for food and water, as they were returning to their homes. Tattered and torn, many of them cruised down the Ashley River on flatboats, squeezed in among the produce that was being floated down river to village markets. York knew Mr. Hampton would be coming home as well. Every day she went out and stood on the balcony of the Manor House and watched for him, just as her Mother had done before her, watching and waiting for the Judge to come riding up.

Mandy huffed and puffed up the stairs with a message for York. Mr. Hampton had sent a telegram stating he would be there on Sunday afternoon, the seventh of April. Cold chills went over Mandy for York was almost the exact image of her mother. If she didn't know better, she would think it was Mrs. Selassie standing there, dressed in gossamer white.

"I's ain't goin' to be able to climb dem' stairs much longer," Mandy said.

"Thank you, Mandy. You should have called me."

"I's couldn't wait fo' you to tell me what it say."

"It says...Mr. Hampton will be here Sunday. Oh Mandy, that's only three days away!"

"Praise be to de' Lord," Mandy cried. "Now I spect' he be as antsy to see you, as you be to see him."

"Mandy, we are going to have a jubilant celebration when he comes marching home!"

Chapter 32

Tray Hampton arrived, just as he said he would, the following Sunday. Tray greeted Victoria and the Colonel in the parlor, and as they excitedly exchanged greetings, his eyes were all the while searching the room for York. She hurriedly descended the stairs and, upon seeing her, Tray rushed to meet her halfway. He took York's white-gloved hands and kissed them with ardor. He wanted to take her in his arms, but he was aware others were looking on. This was not the way it was supposed to be — they wished to be alone. They lingered on the stairway, just studying one another as if they were both in a trance. Mr. Hampton had rid himself of his uniform and was immaculately dressed in a dark frock coat and trousers, as York first remembered him. His hair and the masculine curve of his eyebrows framed his handsome features. York looked into the deep pools of his blue-gray eyes. One could get lost in those eyes and be senseless of any or all surroundings. Tray's hands brushed her cheek and stroked her hair. They finally came to their senses and let Victoria and the Colonel into their private world; a tinge of envy swept over Victoria.

Later in the day, York and Tray retreated to the rose garden.

"At last, my Love, I have you all to myself. I have looked forward to this day for so long."

"The feeling is mutual, Tray."

Tray overshadowed her small frame and drew her close. She met his passionate kiss. Upon releasing York, Tray showered her with yet another declaration of his love. "My darling York, you are my first and only love. I feel so unworthy to claim you as my bride. From the moment you tossed your curls at me and rode away on your dappled mare, I was totally captivated by you."

York blushed. "I suppose your love fell softly on me. I wouldn't admit it, not even to myself; however, you *were* frightfully forward and presumptuous."

"Yes. I bloody well came on a little strong, didn't I? You were a challenge, to say the least. I thought you were beautifully vibrant and alive, unlike the staid and pasty paper dolls with whom I had become acquainted. I treasured every moment we shared together."

"And you, Tray, were my *beau ideal.* When you read Shakespeare's Sonnets to me here in the rose garden, it was as if a whole new world opened for me."

"Then I must applaud Shakespeare, my benefactor."

"Speaking of benefactors, I have one."

"Is that so?" Tray sheepishly inquired.

"Tray, I feel compelled to tell you that the war has been very costly for our family. We almost lost the plantation after Father died. Had it not been for Colonel Bates and our secret benefactor, we would surely have lost everything. I want you to know that you have nothing to gain by marrying me except my love for you."

"Oh York, my Sweet, did you think I would care about wealth, one way or the other?"

"I know your life in England has been far different from ours here in the South."

"Look at me, York, and listen carefully. I don't care about all of that. I, too, have known what it is to struggle and sacrifice for a cause. In my case, I wanted to study law. My parents died of a plague while on a trip to the East Indies. Because of my youth and penury, I was left in an orphanage in India for three years until Uncle Hugh became my legal guardian. He had great ambition for me, but I chose to study law. When he died, I inherited a sizeable sum from him. Your secret benefactor is quite wealthy and he wishes to share his wealth with the love of his life."

York was at a loss for words. She struggled with pride and disbelief. When she fully realized that Tray had been the family's lifeline throughout the worst years of the war, all she could say was, "Oh, Mr. Hampton, you are incorrigible!"

~ ~ ~ ~ ~

York and Tray exchanged their vows in the rose garden with Reverend James Masterson presiding. York did not want a grandiose wedding in spite of Victoria's urging. She and Tray were content to include only a few friends and family members.

Following the modest wedding ceremony, York and Tray bade farewell to well-wishers, and booked passage on a ship sailing to Paris. They spent the larger part of their honeymoon viewing old castles, palatial gardens, and the Louvre; afterward, they visited the Marcellus family and sailed to England. Consumed in their passion for one another, the days passed much too quickly.

When they returned to the low country, Tray set up a law practice in Charleston, and they bought the old Wythe Plantation. Over time, they refurbished the mansion and enlarged the gardens. The renovated Wythe Plantation became one of the showplaces of the South.

In 1870, a son, Tray Hampton, Jr., was born of their union. After the birth of their son, Tray felt the call of God to enter the ministry. He dedicated his life to preaching, teaching, and establishing churches all around the state of South Carolina.

York had also found her purpose in life as a minister's wife. Out of respect for Tray, she always addressed him as *Reverend* Hampton in public, and even among friends. Her southern upbringing and compassion for others brought honor to her husband; and, in turn, their exemplary lives brought glory and honor to God.

~ ~ ~ ~ ~

In their twilight years, they often reminisced and laughed together about the days of their courtship. "York," Tray asked, "do you remember the day I threatened to turn you over my knee and spank you for your insolence?"

"Yes, and I ran straight into the arms of my Father and Colonel Bates, just as they were coming out the door of the Manor House."

"I really wouldn't have hurt you," he said.

"I know. I remember how you wilted and were speechless that day."

"And, I remember the day you shed your petticoats, and kicked them behind the hedge row."

"Oh, Tray, you didn't see me…did you?"

Tray had not seen her, but he had overheard Victoria scolding her over it one day.

"You will never know for sure, will you, my Beloved?"

York looked askance at him. "Oh, Mr. Hampton, you are incorrigible!"

But, York and Tray were both wrong on two counts: York vowed she would never marry Tray, but she did; and Tray vowed he would marry York and ride Duchess — but he never could ride the spirited, dappled mare!